Sabr
the teenage witch
the magic within
book 4

SABRINA THE TEENAGE WITCH: THE MAGIC WITHIN 4
Published by Archie Comic Publications, Inc.
325 Fayette Avenue, Mamaroneck, NY 10543-2318.

FIRST PRINTING. PRINTED IN CANADA.

ISBN: 978-1-936975-76-1

Featuring the Talents of:

STORY	Tania del Rio
PENCILS	Tania del Rio, Lindsay Cibos, Chad Thomas
INKS	Jim Amash
LETTERS	Teresa Davidson, Phil Felix
COVER COLORS	Rosario "Tito" Peña
INTERIOR RENDERING	Jason Jensen, Rosario "Tito" Peña

Characters

SABRINA's life is changing dramatically. Her powers have grown so strong that she is under close scrutiny from the Magic Council, who are worried she may be a threat. That's not good news for **SHINJI** and the growing Four Blades movement . . . They are secretly plotting to overthrow the Queen for allowing the Mana Tree, the source of all the Magic Realm's power, to die.

Trying to escape the drama and pressure, Sabrina decided to give up magic entirely, live a normal, mortal life and date her childhood sweetheart, **HARVEY**. But she soon realized that magic was a part of her, and decided to be completely honest with Harvey about her life as a witch, which brought them closer than ever!

When Sabrina decided to rejoin the Four Blades, she found that her place in the central quartet had been filled by Shinji's new girlfriend, a shady shape-changer named **HEMLOCK**. The Blades gave Sabrina a mission to retrieve a dead leaf from the Mana Tree to prove the truth of their claim about the Queen, and Sabrina succeded, but not without consequences. She traveled to the tree with Harvey, but when they arrived, they spied Hemlock removing dead Mana leaves. What's worse, Hemlock then kissed and left with the mysterious, sinister **VOSBLANC**, the wizard who has been manipulating the Queen, and the real threat to the Magic Realm. Unfortunately, bringing Harvey to the Magic Realm broke one of its strictest laws, forcing the Czarina of Mediation, Sabrina's own **AUNT HILDA**, to erase his memory.

Sabrina is now angry at both worlds and secretly being tutored by a strange old wizard named **"BATTY" BARTHOLEMEW**, from whom she has acquired two ancient, mysterious wands . . .

Chapter 1

THE TURNING PART 1 OF 3

WRITER AND ARTIST: TANIA DEL RIO
INKS: JIM AMASH
COLORS: JASON JENSEN
LETTERS: PHIL FELIX

EDITOR/MANAGING EDITOR: MIKE PELLERITO
EDITOR-IN-CHIEF: VICTOR GORELICK

PREVIOUSLY, SABRINA'S BOYFRIEND HARVEY HAD HIS MEMORY ERASED AFTER GOING WITH HER TO THE MAGIC REALM TO RETRIEVE A MANA LEAF AS PROOF THAT THE MAGIC REALM IS DYING. THIS MISSION WAS FOR THE FOUR BLADES, A GROUP THAT SABRINA'S EX-BOYFRIEND, SHINJI, LEADS, AND WHOSE GOAL IS TO OVERTHROW THE QUEEN AND REVEAL THAT SHE HAS BEEN ALLOWING THE REALM TO DIE UNDER HER WATCH.

IN THE LAST BOOK, SABRINA ACQUIRED TWO MYSTERIOUS WANDS THAT JUST MIGHT COME IN HANDY FOR SHINJI'S CAUSE...
ZAP!
WOAH.

ZAP!
WOOSHH!
SWEET!
ARE YOU STILL PLAYING WITH THOSE THINGS? YOU DON'T EVEN KNOW WHERE THEY'RE FROM!
I TOLD YOU. I GOT THEM AT BATTY BARTHOLOMEW'S YARD SALE! *
* SEE BOOK THREE

YES, BUT WHERE DID HE GET THEM FROM? THOSE WANDS ARE REALLY OLD... I DON'T TRUST THEM!
WHAT ARE YOU SCARED OF? YOU KNOW WANDS ARE POWERLESS ON THEIR OWN! YOU JUST CAN'T STAND TO SEE ME HAVING FUN! I BET YOU'RE GOING TO ENJOY TAKING THESE AWAY FROM ME TOO, HUH?
SABRINA, I KNOW YOU'RE STILL MAD AT ME FOR ERASING HARVEY'S MEMORY AND THAT'S FINE! BUT YOU HAVE TO UNDERSTAND I HAD TO DO IT TO PROTECT US-- AND THE MAGIC REALM!
I'M GETTING TIRED OF YOUR ATTITUDE! I'M STILL YOUR AUNT! SHOW SOME RESPECT!
ZAP!
SLAM!

THESE ARE AMAZING!
HAVE YOU BEEN LEARNING HOW TO USE THEM?
ZAP!
ZAP!
YEAH!
THEY'RE STARTING TO FEEL REALLY GOOD IN MY HANDS... ALMOST LIKE EXTENSIONS OF MY OWN BODY!

THESE WILL REALLY COME IN HANDY FOR FOUR BLADES DAY. BUT DO YOU REALLY NEED BOTH OF THEM?
WHAT?
WELL, IT'S NOT LIKE YOU CAN USE BOTH OF THEM AT THE SAME TIME. MAYBE I SHOULD KEEP ONE. AFTER ALL, I AM THE LEADER OF THIS OPERATION...
I DON'T THINK THAT'S A GOOD IDEA...

COME ON...LET ME JUST TRY ONE OUT REAL QUICK.
FINE.
COME ON, LET GO. I WON'T STEAL IT FROM YOU, I PROMISE.
NICE.

SHAKE!
SHAKE!
SHAKE!
IT'S NOT DOING ANYTHING!
URGH!
COME ON!
WHAT'S THE DEAL?
I HAD THE SAME PROBLEM EARLIER, IT SEEMS THEY DON'T WORK UNLESS YOU HOLD THEM BOTH. THEY CAN'T BE SEPARATED.

IS THAT RIGHT?
SO I GUESS YOU BETTER GIVE IT BACK.
IT'S A SHAME.
WELL, THEN. FINDERS KEEPERS.
THANK YOU.
WELL, THANKS FOR COMING HERE TO SHOW ME THESE. THEY WERE A GOOD FIND! KEEP A CLOSE EYE ON THEM!
I WILL. AND... DON'T TELL HEMLOCK ABOUT THEM, O.K.?

HEY, IF SHE FINDS OUT YOU WERE MEETING ME HERE ALONE, SHE WOULD FLIP OUT! MY LIPS ARE SEALED!
YOU'RE GOING TO TUTORING, RIGHT? I'LL ESCORT YOU THERE. THERE'S BEEN SOME MONSTER SIGHTINGS IN THE AREA.
THEY'VE BEEN SPOTTED EVERY-WHERE IN THE MAGIC REALM.
I'LL BE FINE. I HAVE THE WANDS TO PROTECT ME.
EVEN SO, I'D FEEL BETTER IF YOU JUST LET ME DO THIS.
SURE.

SHINJI? YOU KNOW I DON'T LIKE HEMLOCK AND THAT I DON'T TRUST HER. YOU EVEN ADMITTED TO ME THAT YOU SOMETIMES WONDER ABOUT HER AS WELL.*
* SEE BOOK THREE
SO WHY ARE YOU STILL WITH HER? WHY DO YOU GIVE HER SUCH AN IMPORTANT ROLE IN THE FOUR BLADES WHEN SHE COULD EASILY RUIN EVERYTHING WE'VE WORKED FOR? FOUR BLADES MEANS EVERYTHING TO YOU!
ARE YOU WILLING TO RISK IT ALL FOR A GIRL?
SABRINA... IT'S HARD TO EXPLAIN. YOU BOTH DISLIKE EACH OTHER SO MUCH, ALL YOU SEE IS THE NEGATIVE. BUT I SEE SIDES OF BOTH OF YOU THAT THE OTHER WILL NEVER KNOW.
YES, HEMLOCK IS SECRETIVE. SOMETIMES I DON'T KNOW IF SHE'S BEING TOTALLY HONEST. BUT SHE'S NEVER HAD PEOPLE TRUST IN HER BEFORE. SHE ISN'T USED TO BEING GIVEN RESPONSIBILITY LIKE THIS! THIS IS THE FIRST TIME IN HER LIFE THAT ANYONE HAS GIVEN HER A CHANCE!
AND WHEN IT'S JUST THE TWO OF US, SHE'S A DIFFERENT PERSON. SHE'S FUNNY, SWEET, AND REALLY MOTIVATED. I REALLY LIKE BEING WITH HER. I WISH YOU COULD SEE THIS SIDE OF HER!

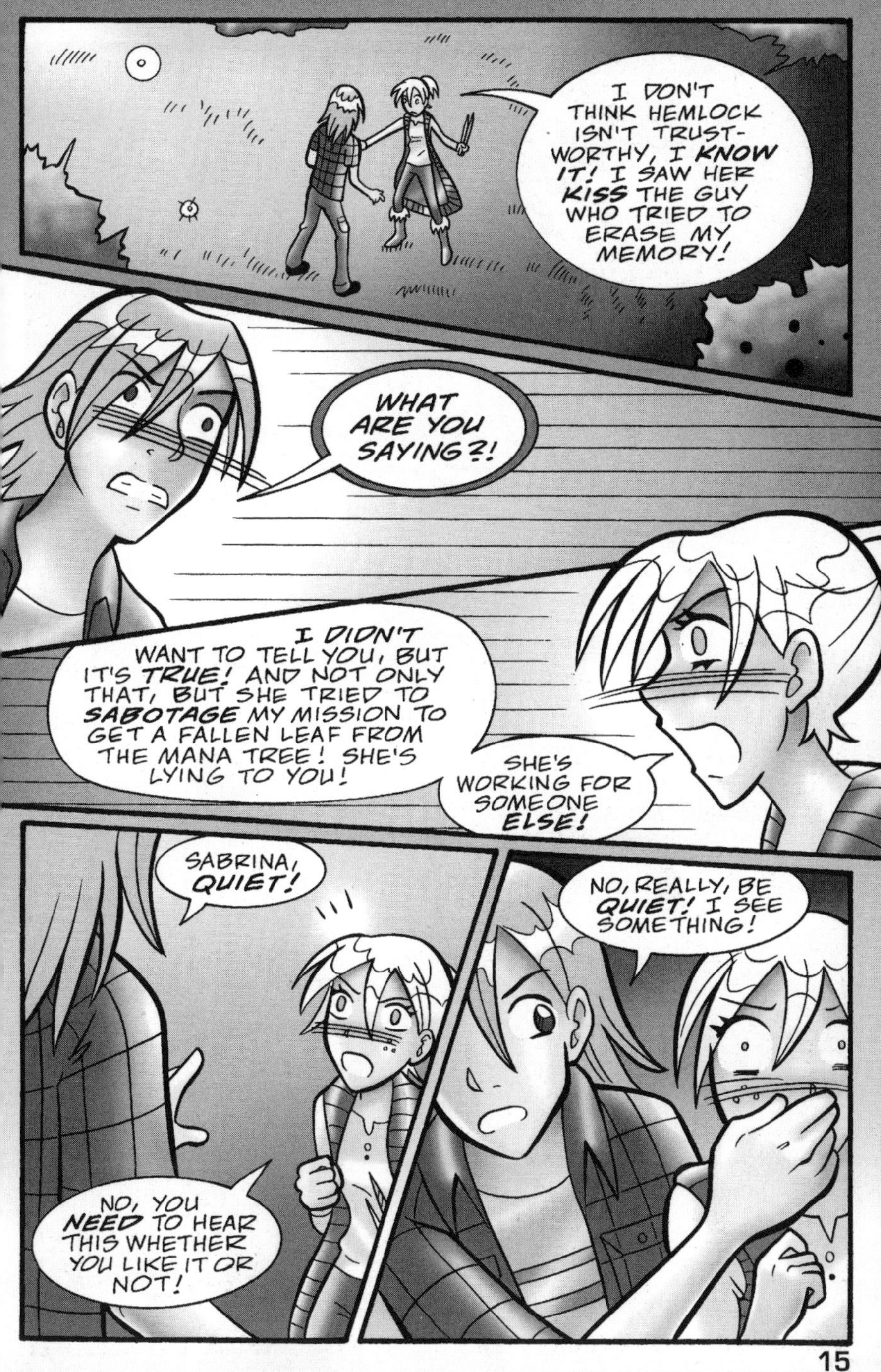
I DON'T THINK HEMLOCK ISN'T TRUST-WORTHY, I KNOW IT! I SAW HER KISS THE GUY WHO TRIED TO ERASE MY MEMORY!
WHAT ARE YOU SAYING?!
I DIDN'T WANT TO TELL YOU, BUT IT'S TRUE! AND NOT ONLY THAT, BUT SHE TRIED TO SABOTAGE MY MISSION TO GET A FALLEN LEAF FROM THE MANA TREE! SHE'S LYING TO YOU!
SHE'S WORKING FOR SOMEONE ELSE!
SABRINA, QUIET!
NO, YOU NEED TO HEAR THIS WHETHER YOU LIKE IT OR NOT!
NO, REALLY, BE QUIET! I SEE SOMETHING!

RUSTLE!
RUSTLE!
SHOULD I USE MY WANDS?
NO... THEY SEEM TO BE PATROLLING. IF THEY SEE US AND SOUND AN ALARM, THERE'LL BE 50 MORE TO DEAL WITH.
THIS IS GETTING INSANE. WHERE DO THEY COME FROM?
I DON'T KNOW, BUT I HAVE A FEELING IT'S ONLY GOING TO GET WORSE.

ONCE AGAIN, I FAIL TO SEE WHAT BATTY BARTHOLOMEW'S LESSON HAS TO DO WITH ANY-THING.
FANTASTIC COOKING

O.K.... I'D UNDERSTAND IT IF YOU WANTED ME TO READ SPELL-BOOKS. BUT THESE ARE COOKBOOKS!
AAAAND?
FANTASTIC COOKING
RECIPES
DINNERTIME
DELISH!

THEY HAVE NOTHING TO DO WITH MAGIC!
BUT THEY DO HAVE TO DO WITH FOOD!

AAAAND?
HAVE YOU DECIDED WHAT WE'RE HAVING FOR DINNER YET?

SIGH!

Ugh... FOR EVERY HOUR I SPEND AT BATTY BARTHOLOMEW'S, I MAYBE LEARN FIVE MINUTES WORTH OF ACTUAL MAGIC!

STILL...THE OLD LOONY IS STARTING TO GROW ON ME!
CRACKLE!
I WISH SHINJI WERE HERE NOW... IT'S GETTING LATE AND WHO KNOWS WHAT'S IN THIS FOREST!
AND BEING UNABLE TO USE MY MAGIC HERE DOESN'T MAKE ME FEEL ANY SAFER.
Ah!

O.K. ...DON'T PANIC. HE'S FAR AWAY. JUST KEEP MOVING.
GRRRRRRGGGHHH
AH!
TRIP!

FIZZLE!
NNGGGH!
GRRRR
IT'S NO USE! I HAVE NO MAGIC HERE!
BLAST!

OH, THANK GOODNESS! THE WANDS WORK HERE! BUT HOW? THEY'RE NOT SUPPOSED TO HAVE ANY POWER OF THEIR OWN!
SIZZLE!

AND NOT ONLY DO THEY WORK, BUT THEY'RE SUPER STRONG!
A SECRET PASSAGE?

Woah!

I AM SO COMING BACK! THIS WAND MAY BE SUPER POWERFUL, BUT WITH ALL THESE MONSTERS IN THE AREA, IT'S PROBABLY BETTER TO WAIT...
REPAIR

MAYBE I CAN GET SHINJI AND LLANDRA TO GO BACK TO THE CAVE WITH ME...

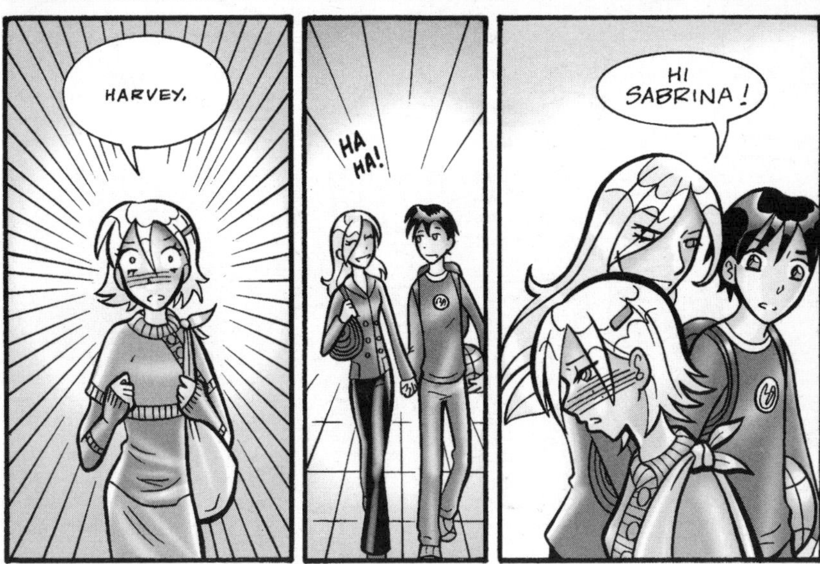
HARVEY.
HA HA!
HI SABRINA!

WHO'S THAT?
OUCH, HARVEY! THAT'S HARSH, EVEN BY MY STANDARDS!
I'M SO GLAD YOU INVITED ME ON A GIRLS' NIGHT OUT, LLANDRA! I CAN'T TELL YOU HOW MUCH I NEED IT!
AW, WELL... I MISS OUR ONE-ON-ONE TIME!
AND I FIGURED YOU MIGHT WANT TO GET YOUR MIND OFF HARVEY AND AMY...
YEAH...
NEVER MIND THAT! TELL ME MORE ABOUT THIS CAVE YOU FOUND TODAY!

OH, IT WAS SO AMAZING! I REALIZED THIS WAND CAN BREAK THROUGH ANYTHING! I SEALED IT UP AFTER I LEFT, BUT I REMEMBER WHERE IT WAS!
GIRL, ARE YOU CRAZY? PUT THOSE THINGS AWAY!
WHAT? THEY'RE JUST STICKS.
THEY ARE NOT STICKS AND YOU KNOW IT. WOULD YOU PULL DAGGERS OUT IN THE MIDDLE OF YOUR PEDICURE? I DON'T THINK SO!
OH, WHATEVER! I JUST LIKE HOLDING THEM! THEY MAKE ME FEEL SO CALM...
LATER...
ARE YOU READY TO CHALLENGE ME OR ARE YOU JUST GOING TO PLAY WITH YOUR WANDS ALL NIGHT?

SORRRRY! I GUESS I'M EASILY DISTRACTED!
I'LL SAY!
YOU KNOW, YOU SHOULD PROBABLY BE MORE CAREFUL WITH THOSE IF THEY'RE AS POWERFUL AS YOU SAY THEY ARE!
GRAB
DON'T TOUCH THEM!
EASY! I WAS JUST LOOKING. RELAX!
SORRY... I DON'T KNOW WHAT'S WRONG WITH ME!
IT'S FINE. CAN WE JUST PLAY THE GAME ALREADY?

SABRINA IS STARTING TO ACT **VERY** STRANGE!

ARE THE **WANDS** HAVING SOME **DARK** EFFECT ON HER PERSONALITY?

. . . AND WHAT WILL HAPPEN IF SOMEONE TRIES TO TAKE THE WANDS **AWAY**?

Chapter 2

The TURNING
~PART 2 OF 3~
WRITER & ARTIST • TANIA DEL RIO
INKS • JIM AMASH
COLORS • JASON JENSEN
LETTERS • TERESA DAVIDSON
EDITOR/MANAGING EDITOR
MIKE PELLERITO
EDITOR-IN-CHIEF
VICTOR GORELICK
SABRINA!
HEY! SABRINA! OVER HERE!
H-HARVEY?

HARVEY! YOU REMEMBER ME!
REMEMBER YOU? HOW COULD I EVER FORGET?

EXCUSE ME!
THAT'S MY BOYFRIEND YOU'RE KISSING!
LET'S GO, HARVEY!
WAIT! LET HIM GO!
HARVEY!!

HARVEY... NO...
AMY... DON'T...
TWITCH
CRACKLE
CRACKLE

MORNING, SUNSHINE. YOU LOOK A MESS. EVERYTHING OK?
NO! I HAVE THE WORST HEADACHE!
POP CRUNCH

WELL, GET SOME BREAKFAST IN YOU AND I'M SURE YOU'LL FEEL BETTER.
Nah... I'M NOT HUNGRY.
POP CRUNCH
NOT... HUNGRY?!
WHAT DOES THAT EVEN MEAN?

ARE YOU SURE YOU'RE FEELING OK?
DO YOU NEED TO STAY HOME FROM SCHOOL?
I'M FINE!
GEEZ.
...

WELL, YOU GUYS ARE BORING, SO I GUESS I'M GOING TO GO TO SCHOOL NOW.
WELL, EXCUSE ME!
POP CRUNCH
SOMEONE GOT UP ON THE WRONG SIDE OF THE BED!
SHE HASN'T BEEN HERSELF LATELY...
WELL, SHE IS A TEENAGER.
STILL... SOMETHING ISN'T RIGHT.
OFF TO SCHOOL ALREADY?
OFF TO ERASE MORE MEMORIES?
THAT'S ENOUGH. YOU HAVE BEEN EXTREMELY DISRESPECTFUL LATELY!
WHATEVER.
THAT'S IT!
YOU'RE GROUNDED!

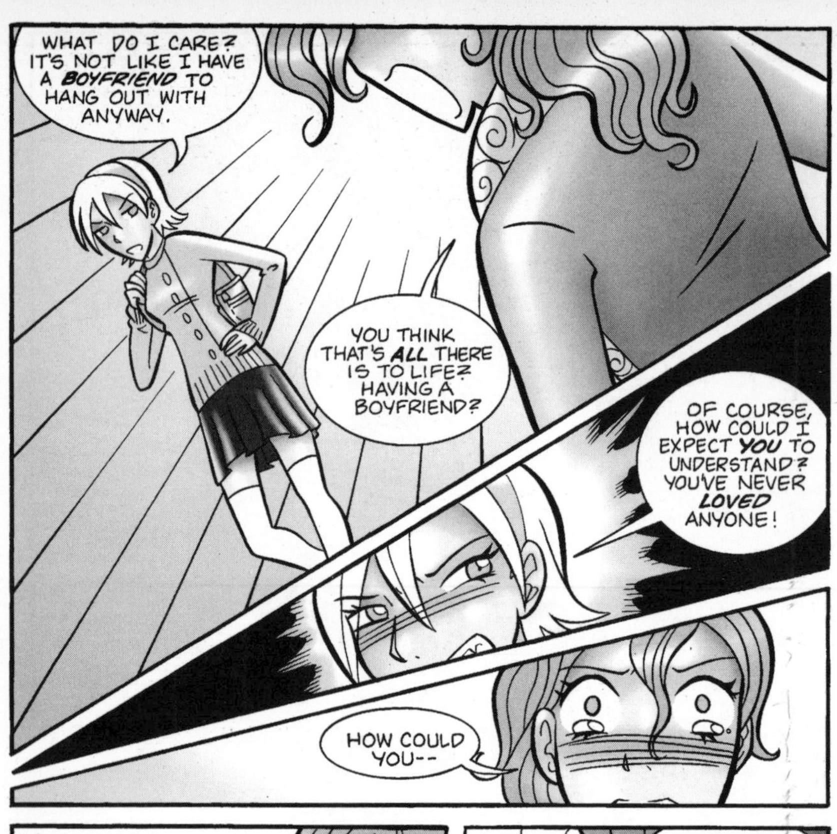
WHAT DO I CARE? IT'S NOT LIKE I HAVE A BOYFRIEND TO HANG OUT WITH ANYWAY.
YOU THINK THAT'S ALL THERE IS TO LIFE? HAVING A BOYFRIEND?
OF COURSE, HOW COULD I EXPECT YOU TO UNDERSTAND? YOU'VE NEVER LOVED ANYONE!
HOW COULD YOU--

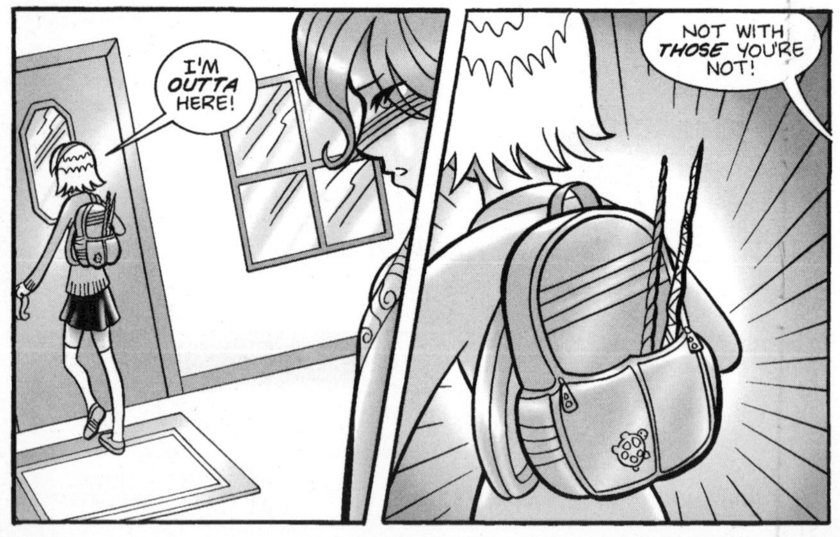
I'M OUTTA HERE!
NOT WITH THOSE YOU'RE NOT!

NO!
NO! I'M NOT GOING TO LET YOU BRING WANDS TO YOUR MORTAL HIGH SCHOOL!
GIVE THOSE BACK!
SABRINA, LET GO THIS INSTANT!
NO! THEY'RE MINE!
WHAT ON EARTH IS GOING ON HERE?!
ZAP

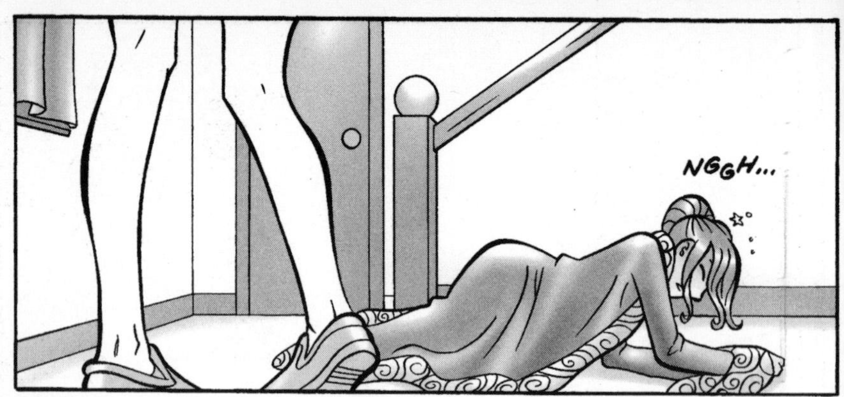
NGGH...

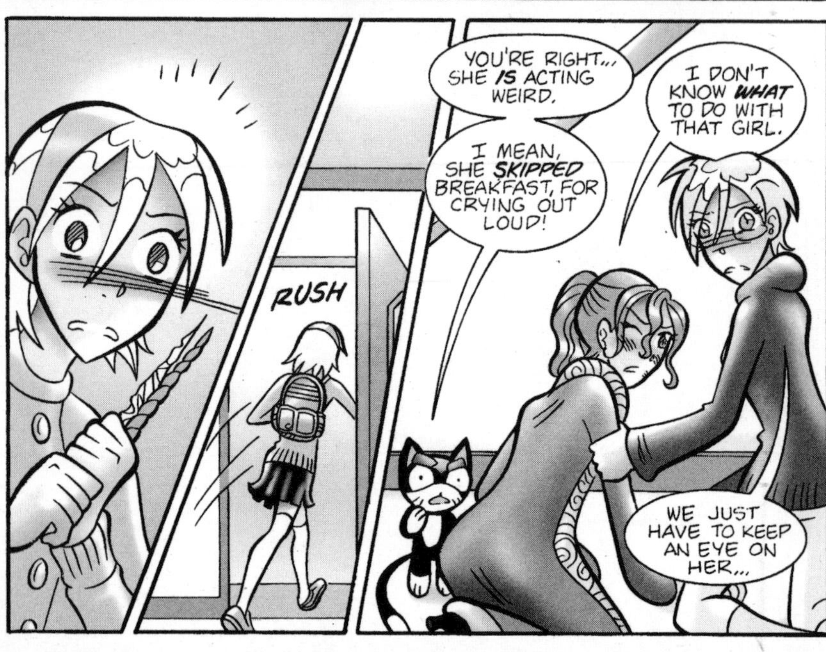
RUSH
YOU'RE RIGHT... SHE IS ACTING WEIRD.
I MEAN, SHE SKIPPED BREAKFAST, FOR CRYING OUT LOUD!
I DON'T KNOW WHAT TO DO WITH THAT GIRL.
WE JUST HAVE TO KEEP AN EYE ON HER...

I DON'T KNOW WHAT GOT INTO ME...
I CAN'T BELIEVE I ZAPPED HILDA. I'M GONNA BE IN SOOO MUCH TROUBLE WHEN I GET HOME...
BUT SHE SHOULDN'T HAVE TRIED TAKING MY WANDS!
THEY'RE MINE!

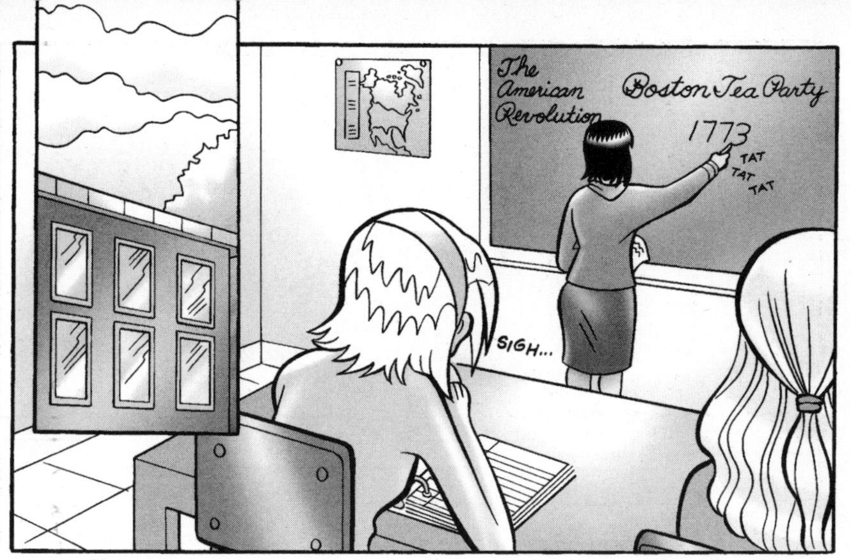
The American Revolution
Boston Tea Party
1773
TAT TAT TAT
SIGH...

TAT
Huh?

Four Blades meeting tonite. you in?
can't. grounded

SABRINA, ARE YOU SERIOUSLY GROUNDED?
YEAH... BIG TIME.
FOR WHAT?
FOR TALKING BACK TO HILDA... AND ZAPPING HER.

WHAT?!
SLAM
LOOK, I'D RATHER NOT TALK ABOUT IT.
SUIT YOURSELF. ANYWAY, WE HAVE GYM CLASS TOGETHER, RIGHT? I'LL WALK WITH YOU.

Uggh, I ALMOST FORGOT. TODAY WE'RE SWITCHING FROM SOCCER TO GYMNASTICS.
SO?

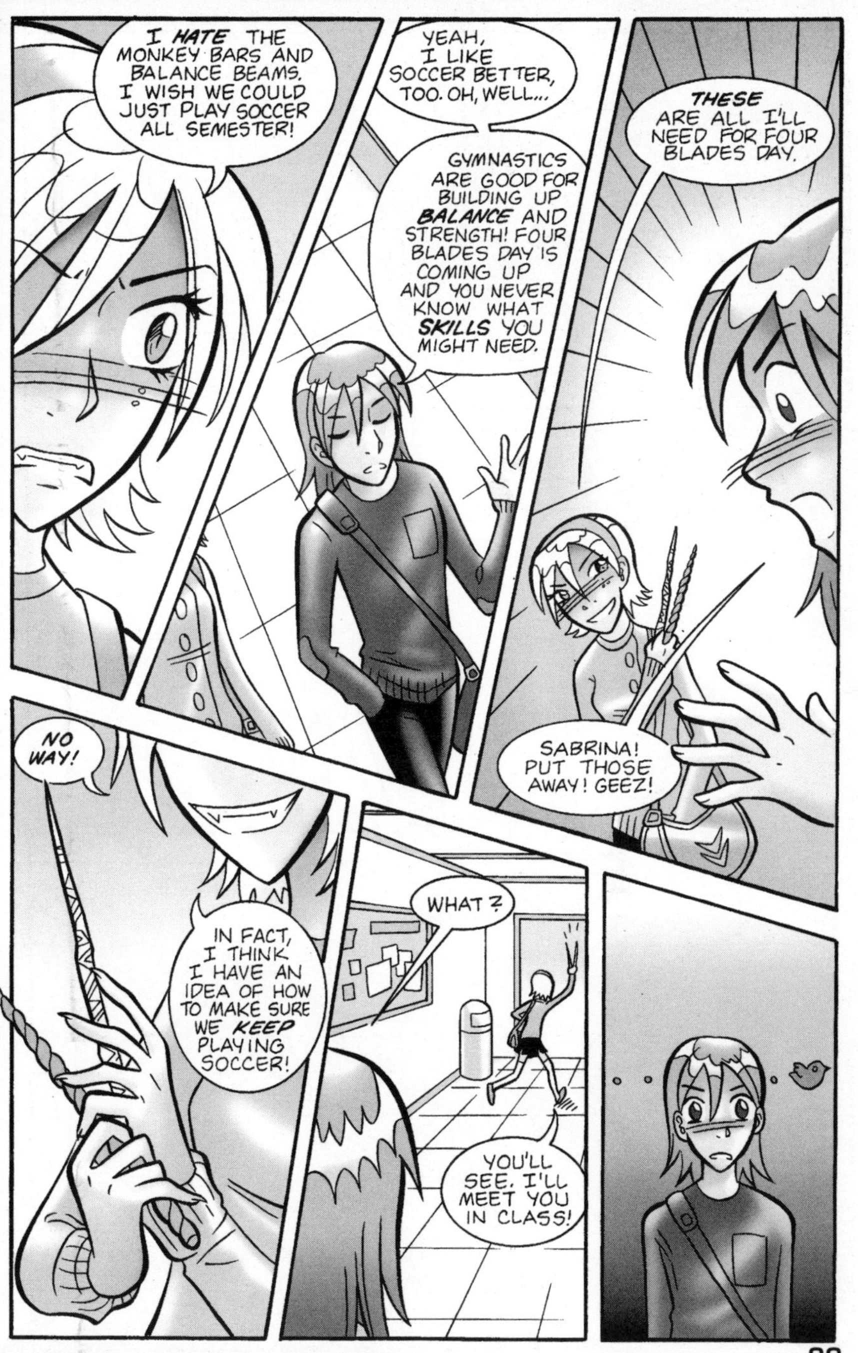
I HATE THE MONKEY BARS AND BALANCE BEAMS. I WISH WE COULD JUST PLAY SOCCER ALL SEMESTER!
YEAH, I LIKE SOCCER BETTER, TOO. OH, WELL...
GYMNASTICS ARE GOOD FOR BUILDING UP BALANCE AND STRENGTH! FOUR BLADES DAY IS COMING UP AND YOU NEVER KNOW WHAT SKILLS YOU MIGHT NEED.
THESE ARE ALL I'LL NEED FOR FOUR BLADES DAY.
SABRINA! PUT THOSE AWAY! GEEZ!
NO WAY!
IN FACT, I THINK I HAVE AN IDEA OF HOW TO MAKE SURE WE KEEP PLAYING SOCCER!
WHAT?
YOU'LL SEE. I'LL MEET YOU IN CLASS!

HEH HEH
Hmmm...
SNEAK
ZAP!!
WAAHH!!!

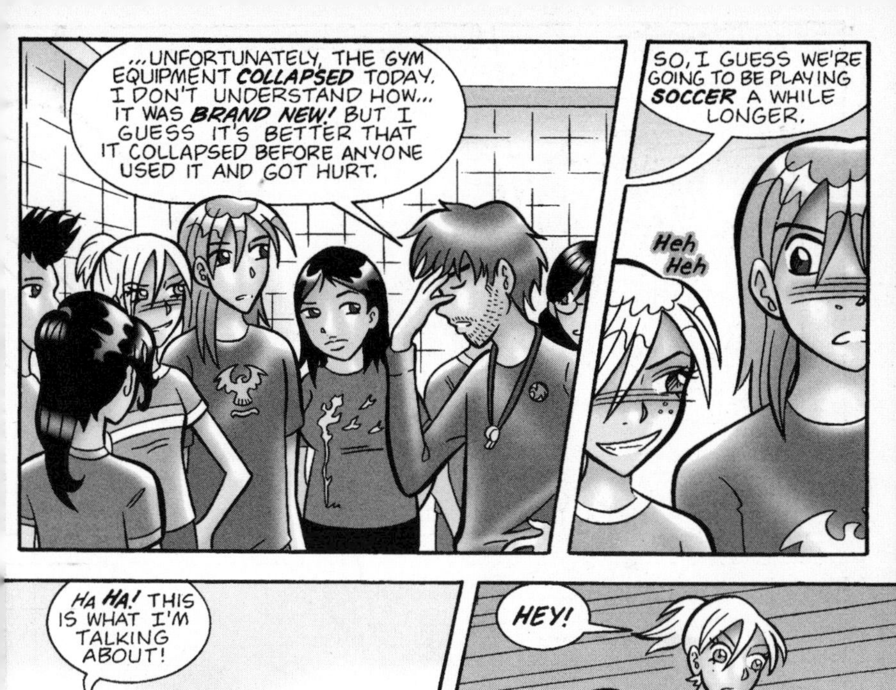
...UNFORTUNATELY, THE GYM EQUIPMENT COLLAPSED TODAY. I DON'T UNDERSTAND HOW... IT WAS BRAND NEW! BUT I GUESS IT'S BETTER THAT IT COLLAPSED BEFORE ANYONE USED IT AND GOT HURT.
SO, I GUESS WE'RE GOING TO BE PLAYING SOCCER A WHILE LONGER.
Heh Heh

HA HA! THIS IS WHAT I'M TALKING ABOUT!
HEY!
FWAP
GO SHINJI!
SHOOT IT!

LET'S SEE HOW YOUR SOCCER SKILLS STAND UP TO MY WANDS!
ZAP
I'VE GOT THIS ONE IN THE BAG!
POW

WHAT THE--!
WHOA! YOU'RE STRONG, SHINJI!

WHAT IS GOING ON TODAY?

HA HA HA HA HA HA HA HA HA HA

WHAT THE HECK IS YOUR PROBLEM, SABRINA?
OH, RELAX. IT WAS JUST A JOKE.

YOU KNOW WHAT? IT'S A GOOD THING YOU'RE GROUNDED. I WOULDN'T WANT YOU TO COME TO THE MEETING TONIGHT ANYWAY. NOT WHEN YOU'RE ACTING LIKE THIS!
SABRINA! CLASS ISN'T OVER YET! WHERE ARE YOU GOING?
STOMP STOMP

FORGET SHINJI AND HIS STUPID MEETING! AND FORGET GYM CLASS!
LATER, AMY.
ARE WE STILL UP FOR A WALK IN THE PARK TONIGHT?
I WOULDN'T MISS IT FOR THE WORLD.
NO.

I DON'T FEEL WELL...
I THINK I NEED TO GO HOME.

I HAD A FEELING YOU WERE SICK.
JUST TAKE IT EASY, OK? GET SOME REST.
AM I STILL GROUNDED?
SORRY, HON. DOCTOR'S ORDERS.
AW, COME ON...
I'M SORRY, SABRINA. I KNOW YOU'RE NOT FEELING WELL, BUT THAT DOESN'T GIVE YOU THE RIGHT TO TREAT HILDA THE WAY YOU DID.
IN FACT, HILDA AND I ARE WORRIED ABOUT YOU.
WE'VE DECIDED TO PUT UP A MAGIC BARRIER WHILE YOU'RE GROUNDED. IT'S FOR YOUR OWN SAFETY.
WHAT?! YOU CAN'T DO THAT!
SORRY, 'BRINA. JUST TRY AND GET SOME REST.
YOU'RE TREATING ME LIKE A PRISONER!
ARE YOU SCARED OF ME OR SOMETHING?

WELL YOU SHOULD BE AFRAID!
I'M MORE POWERFUL THAN YOU! I CAN BREAK THROUGH YOUR BARRIER IF I WANTED TO! I CAN DO WHATEVER I WANT!
JUST TRY AND STOP ME.
SO IS EVERYONE CLEAR ON THEIR TASKS?
WE'RE GOING TO HAVE A RALLY SOON AND GET OUR SUPPORTERS TOGETHER. IT'S GOING TO BE RISKY TO HAVE EVERYONE IN ONE PLACE, BUT IT WILL BE GOOD FOR MORALE.

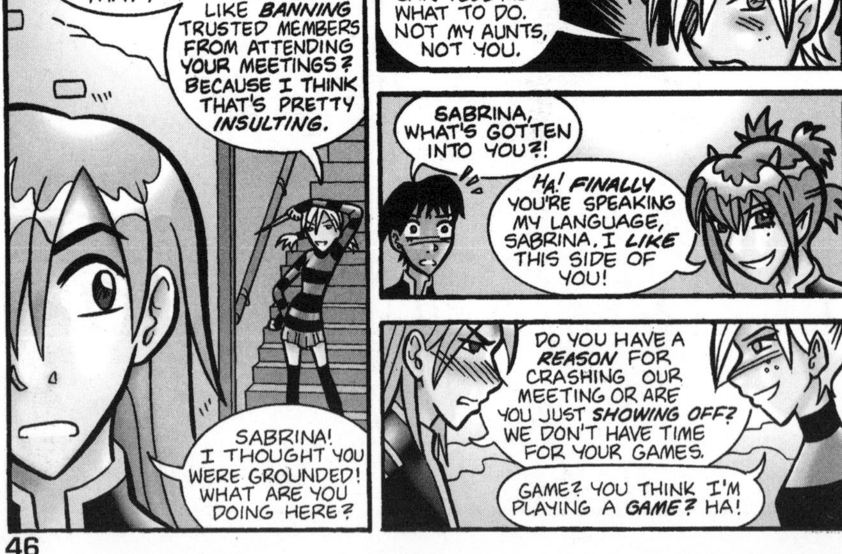
MORALE? WHAT'S THAT?
IS THAT LIKE BANNING TRUSTED MEMBERS FROM ATTENDING YOUR MEETINGS? BECAUSE I THINK THAT'S PRETTY INSULTING.
SABRINA! I THOUGHT YOU WERE GROUNDED! WHAT ARE YOU DOING HERE?
NO ONE CAN TELL ME WHAT TO DO. NOT MY AUNTS, NOT YOU.
SABRINA, WHAT'S GOTTEN INTO YOU?!
HA! FINALLY YOU'RE SPEAKING MY LANGUAGE, SABRINA. I LIKE THIS SIDE OF YOU!
DO YOU HAVE A REASON FOR CRASHING OUR MEETING OR ARE YOU JUST SHOWING OFF? WE DON'T HAVE TIME FOR YOUR GAMES.
GAME? YOU THINK I'M PLAYING A GAME? HA!

I CAME HERE TO WARN YOU, SHINJI.
DON'T GET ON MY BAD SIDE. I HAVE A LOT OF POWER AND I'M WILLING TO SHARE IT WITH YOU AND YOUR CAUSE, BUT ONLY IF YOU TREAT ME WITH THE RESPECT I DESERVE.
SHOOP
NOW, IF YOU'LL EXCUSE ME, I HAVE TO TAKE CARE OF SOMETHING I SHOULD HAVE DEALT WITH EARLIER.
WHAT ARE YOU GOING TO DO?
DON'T LET THE PORTAL CLOSE! FOLLOW HER!
POOF
RUSH
HEMLOCK!
SHOOOP

NARAYAN! I'M SCARED! WHAT'S GOING ON WITH SABRINA?
I DON'T KNOW... LET'S JUST HOPE SHINJI CAN BRING HER TO HER SENSES!
I'M SO HAPPY, HARVEY! I CAN'T TELL YOU HOW LONG I'VE WANTED THIS!
ME TOO, AMY! I CAN'T BELIEVE IT'S TAKEN US THIS LONG TO GET TOGETHER. I MUST HAVE HAD A GOOD REASON FOR NOT ASKING YOU OUT SOONER... I GUESS I WAS JUST SHY!

WITH THIS WAND I CAN DESTROY ANYTHING, EVEN RELATIONSHIPS. THIS WILL TEACH AMY TO TAKE WHAT BELONGS TO ME!
THERE SHE IS!

ZAP
SABRINA! NO!
GET OFF ME!
UNGH!
WHAT'S WRONG?
YOU'RE WHAT'S WRONG! I HATE YOU! GET AWAY FROM ME!
HA HA HA HA HA HA HA HA HA HA HA HA

IT LOOKS LIKE THINGS HAVE GONE FROM **BAD** TO **WORSE**.

SABRINA IS ACTING TOTALLY **EVIL!**

IS IT TOO LATE TO PULL HER OUT OF THE **DARK PLACE** THE WANDS HAVE TAKEN HER?

Chapter 3

THE TURNING PART 3 of 3
WAAAAHH!!..
WRITER TANIA DEL RIO
PENCILLER LINDSAY CIBOS
INKS · JIM AMASH
COLORS · JASON JENSEN
LETTERS · TERESA DAVIDSON
EDITOR & MANAGING EDITOR MIKE PELLERITO
EDITOR-IN-CHIEF VICTOR GORELICK

SALEM! WHAT'S WRONG?
DO YOU REALLY NEED TO ASK?!
IT'S SABRINA! SHE JUST ZAPPED ME FOR TRYING TO NAP ON HER BED!

THAT'S IT... THIS HAS GONE TOO FAR.
I'M GOING TO HAVE TO REPORT HER TO THE MAGIC COUNCIL. THEY'LL HAVE TO TAKE HER INTO CUSTODY.

HILDA, NO!
SHE'S OUR NIECE! SHE'S ONLY 16! THE MAGIC COUNCIL ALREADY DISTRUSTS SABRINA AND HER POWERS... IF YOU REPORT HER, WE MAY NEVER SEE HER AGAIN!

I DON'T KNOW WHAT ELSE TO DO! SHE'S ALREADY ZAPPED ME ONCE, AND NOW SALEM! SHE'S OUT OF CONTROL!
IF WE LET HER CARRY ON, SHE'LL END UP REALLY HURTING SOMEONE! OR GETTING ARRESTED BY THE MORTAL POLICE!

THIS ISN'T SABRINA, IT'S THOSE WANDS SHE HAS! IF SHE COULD JUST LET THEM GO!
GOOD LUCK TRYING TO GET THEM FROM HER! SHE GOES BALLISTIC IF THEY'RE OUT OF HER SIGHT! SHE EVEN SLEEPS WITH THEM IN HER GRASP!

WE CAN'T LET THIS CONTINUE. SABRINA IS HOLDING US HOSTAGE IN OUR OWN HOME! FAMILY OR NOT, WE'RE GOING TO HAVE TO TURN HER IN UNLESS WE FIGURE OUT ANOTHER SOLUTION!

MAN, I'M BOOOOORRED!

BUT WHAT TO DO? I'VE ALREADY REDECORATED MY LAME ROOM AND PLAYED PRANKS ON SALEM. I'VE TRIED CALLING LLANDRA, BUT SHE'S NOT AROUND.

MAYBE I SHOULD TAKE MY BROOM ON A LITTLE LATE NIGHT JOYRIDE!

Heh. SO HILDA'S PUT MAGICAL BARRIERS ALL OVER THE HOUSE. DOES SHE HONESTLY THINK THEY CAN STOP ME FROM LEAVING?

SHINJI?
WELL, WELL! THIS SHOULD ADD SOME EXCITEMENT TO MY DULL EVENING!

SHINJI? IT'S LATE! WHAT ARE YOU DOING HERE?
I NEED TO SEE SABRINA.

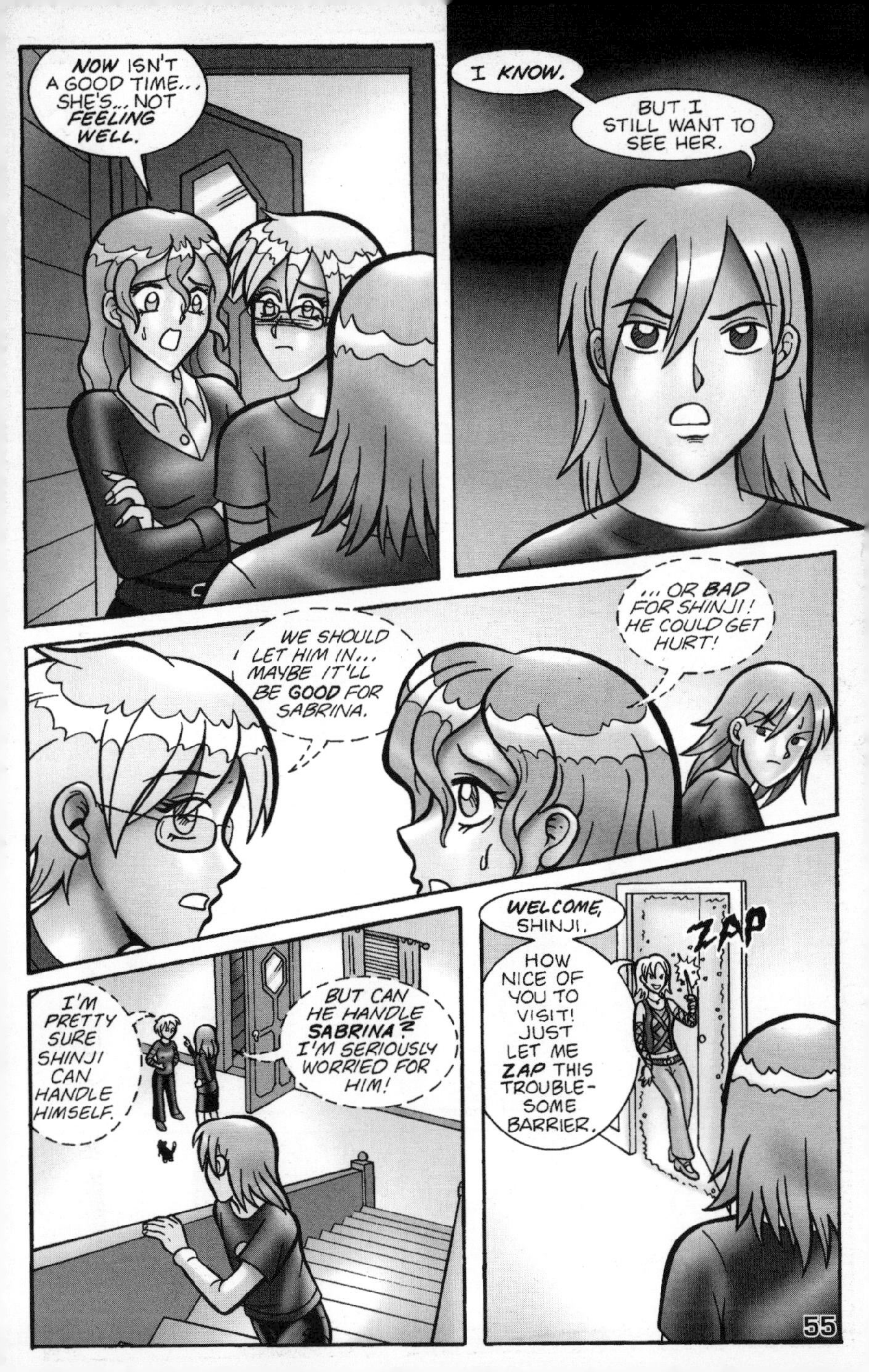
NOW ISN'T A GOOD TIME... SHE'S... NOT FEELING WELL.
I KNOW.
BUT I STILL WANT TO SEE HER.
WE SHOULD LET HIM IN... MAYBE IT'LL BE GOOD FOR SABRINA.
...OR BAD FOR SHINJI! HE COULD GET HURT!
I'M PRETTY SURE SHINJI CAN HANDLE HIMSELF.
BUT CAN HE HANDLE SABRINA? I'M SERIOUSLY WORRIED FOR HIM!
WELCOME, SHINJI.
HOW NICE OF YOU TO VISIT! JUST LET ME ZAP THIS TROUBLE-SOME BARRIER.
ZAP

SO, ARE YOU HERE TO BEG FORGIVENESS? YOU'RE LUCKY I'M EVEN WILLING TO TALK TO YOU. I DIDN'T LIKE HOW YOU TRIED TO SHUT ME OUT OF YOUR FOUR BLADES MEETING LAST WEEK.*
* SEE LAST CHAPTER
THE LEAF.
GIVE IT TO ME.

LEAF?
WHAT LEAF?

DON'T PLAY GAMES WITH ME.
THE DYING MANA LEAF THAT YOU RETRIEVED ON YOUR MISSION. HAND IT OVER.
WHY?

BECAUSE I DON'T TRUST YOU ANYMORE.

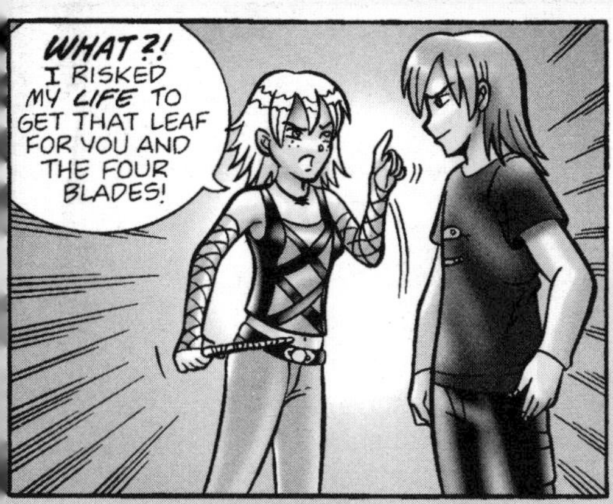
WHAT?! I RISKED MY LIFE TO GET THAT LEAF FOR YOU AND THE FOUR BLADES!

YOU WERE DIFFERENT THEN.

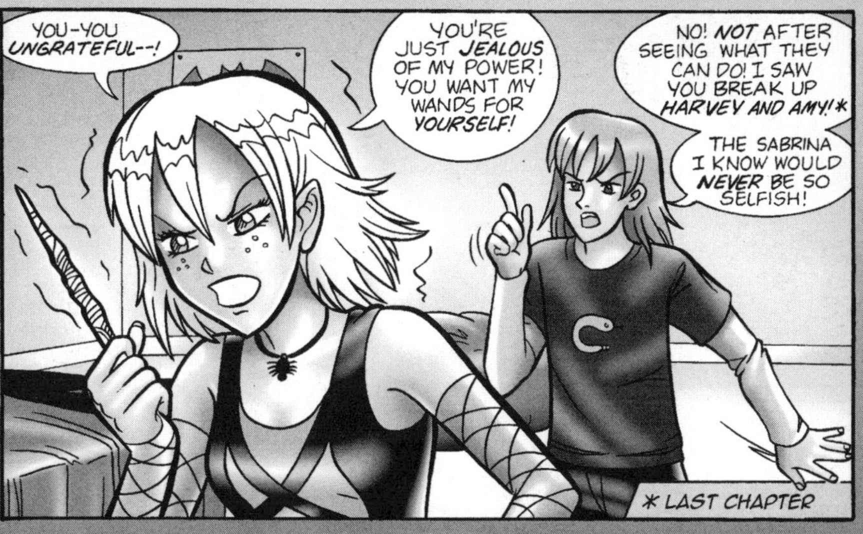
YOU-YOU UNGRATEFUL--!
YOU'RE JUST JEALOUS OF MY POWER! YOU WANT MY WANDS FOR YOURSELF!
NO! NOT AFTER SEEING WHAT THEY CAN DO! I SAW YOU BREAK UP HARVEY AND AMY!*
THE SABRINA I KNOW WOULD NEVER BE SO SELFISH!
* LAST CHAPTER

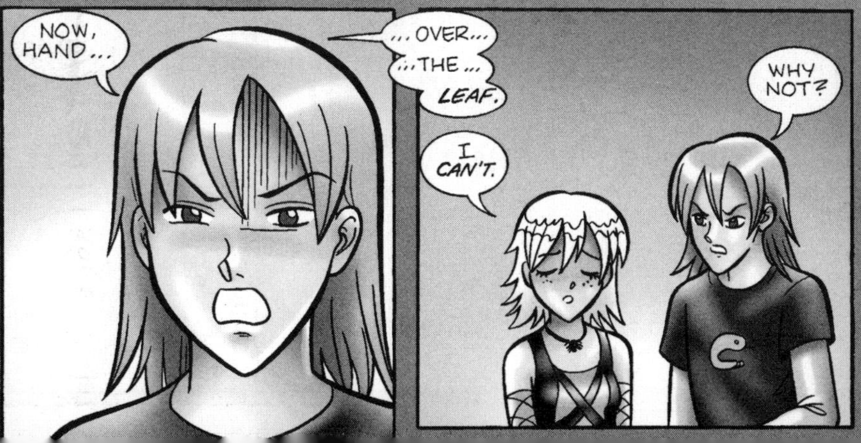
NOW, HAND...
...OVER...
...THE...
LEAF.
WHY NOT?
I CAN'T.

IT'S *GONE.*
WHAAAAT?!
WHERE IS IT?
ASK YOUR *GIRLFRIEND,* HEMLOCK!
SHE HAS SOMETHING TO DO WITH ITS DISAPPEARANCE, I *KNOW* IT!

THAT LEAF WAS THE *ONLY* SOLID *PROOF* WE HAD TO SHOW THAT THE *QUEEN* IS ALLOWING THE MAGIC REALM TO DIE.
WITHOUT IT, THE FOUR BLADES HAVE *NOTHING.*

YOU... *FAILED* ME, SABRINA.

HA!
WHEN WILL SHINJI LEARN TO SEE HEMLOCK FOR WHO SHE REALLY IS? IT'S NOT MY FAULT THE LEAF'S MISSING! I DID MY PART OF THE BARGAIN!
WHATEVER.

HE HAS TO BE AROUND HERE, SOMEWHERE...
UP... THERE.
O MIGHTY, TWISTING VINES. BEND DOWN TO ME AND CARRY ME UP THIS CLIFF.
OH... RIGHT...
I'M IN A MAGIC FOREST. MY SPELLS DON'T WORK HERE.
WELL, AT LEAST MY HANDS STILL WORK.

YES! I MADE IT!

BATTY BARTHOLOMEW!
KNOCK
KNOCK

WOOSH
SIGH

SABRINA IS YOUR STUDENT! HOW CAN YOU NOT BE AWARE OF WHAT'S BEEN GOING ON?
Er... WHAT'S BEEN GOING ON?
SHE'S TURNED EVIL!
IT'S THOSE WANDS SHE HAS! THEY HAVE SOMETHING TO DO WITH IT, I KNOW IT!
...AAND?

YOU'RE HER MENTOR! YOU'RE RESPONSIBLE FOR HER MAGICAL EDUCATION! SHE'S RUNNING WILD, CAUSING DESTRUCTION! DON'T YOU CARE?
OH, DEAR. THAT IS A PICKLE. WELL, WHAT SHOULD WE DO?
THAT'S WHAT I CAME TO ASK YOU! YOU'RE THE EXPERT! HOW DO WE FIX THIS?

Hmmm...

AH!

I MAY HAVE JUST THE THING!

TA-DA!
SIGH
WHAT IS THAT?
DUCT TAPE! I HEAR IT CAN FIX ANYTHING!
ALRIGHT. I GUESS IT'S UP TO ME, THEN.
I'M JUST GOING TO HAVE TO TRY AND REASON WITH HER, AS IMPOSSIBLE AS THAT SOUNDS.
Hmm... THAT COULD BE RISKY.
YOU'D BETTER TAKE THIS.

A BATTERY?! WHAT GOOD WILL THIS DO ME?
POWER AA
WELL... IT'S LONG LASTING!
SIGH... THIS WAS A WASTE OF TIME.
WHY DID I THINK BATTY BARTHOLOMEW WOULD BE ABLE TO HELP?
WELL, uh... THANKS FOR THE BATTERY. I GUESS I'LL BE OFF NOW.
WAIT A MINUTE!
THAT'S IT!
I THINK WE MAY BE ABLE TO SAVE SABRINA AFTER ALL!

SLEEP IS FOR THE **WEAK!** LET'S SHAKE THINGS UP!
ICE LUSO

WEEEEEE
BLAST!
BOOM
BOOM
BOOM
HAHA HAHA
HA
HA

SLURRRRRP
Bah. REFILL TIME.

Sabrina Spellman, I bring you a magical message from **Llandra** Da Silva!
WHAT THE--!!

SHE CAN'T JUST CALL ME ON MY **CELL**? WHAT'S WITH THIS **SHOW-OFFY** MAGIC?

Llandra challenges you to a duel!
She claims your **wands** cannot stand up to her powerful **plant magic**.
If you are not afraid to take this challenge, she will meet you tomorrow in the Charm School **greenhouse** at noon!

SHE CHALLENGES ME?! WHO DOES SHE THINK SHE IS?
NO TRUE FRIEND OF MINE WOULD QUESTION MY POWER!
ZAP
WHAT IF SHE DOESN'T SHOW?

NO, SHE HAS TO! SHE'S TOO POWER-HUNGRY TO REFUSE A CHALLENGE, EVEN IF THAT CHALLENGE IS JUST BAIT TO GET HER HERE!

Uh, BATTY? DON'T TOUCH THAT-- IT'S POISONOUS.

WELL, WELL, WELL. I GUESS YOU IMAGINE YOU HAVE SOME KIND OF ADVANTAGE HAVING A DUEL IN THE MIDDLE OF A GREENHOUSE, hmm?
BUT IF MY WAND DESTROYS ALL THE PLANTS, YOU WON'T HAVE ANYTHING TO HELP YOU!
SABRINA, LISTEN TO ME. I BROUGHT YOU HERE SO I COULD TELL YOU SOMETHING IMPORTANT!
SAVE THE TALKING FOR AFTER OUR DUEL! I WANT TO GIVE YOU A TASTE OF MY POWER!

I DIDN'T COME HERE TO *DUEL* YOU. I CAME HERE TO TALK TO YOU! ABOUT YOUR WANDS!
WELL, THAT'S *TOO BAD*...
BLAST
ZAP
...BECAUSE *I* CAME HERE TO *DUEL* YOU!
UNNGH!
LISTEN TO ME!

JUST LIKE THIS BATTERY, YOUR WANDS ARE BOTH POSITIVE AND NEGATIVE!
YOU'RE BORING ME!

IT'S ALL ABOUT BALANCE, SABRINA!
YOU'VE BEEN USING THE DESTRUCTIVE WAND TOO MUCH! YOU HAVE TO USE THE WANDS EQUALLY, OR NOT AT ALL!
ARE YOU GOING TO FIGHT ME OR NOT?

FINE!
I'LL DEFEAT YOU IF THAT'S WHAT IT TAKES TO MAKE YOU LISTEN!

YOUR PLANTS ARE NO MATCH FOR ME, LLANDRA! THEY'RE WEAK!
NGH!
ARGGH!
LET GO!

PUT... ME... DOWN!
THIS ISN'T FAIR!
MY WAAANDS!!
GIVE THEM BACK!
NOT UNTIL YOU HEAR ME OUT!
YOU NEED TO START USING THE REGENERATION WAND TO COUNTER THE EFFECTS OF THE DESTRUCTION WAND, UNDERSTAND? USE IT TO HEAL! USE IT FOR GOOD! IT'S ABOUT BALANCE!
WHAT... HAVE I DONE?

THAT DARK WAND WAS GETTING TOO MUCH CONTROL OVER YOU. YOU CAN'T USE IT ANYMORE! ONLY THE REGENERATION WAND!
I'M SCARED. I DON'T WANT TO TOUCH THEM AGAIN. THEY'LL OVERTAKE ME.

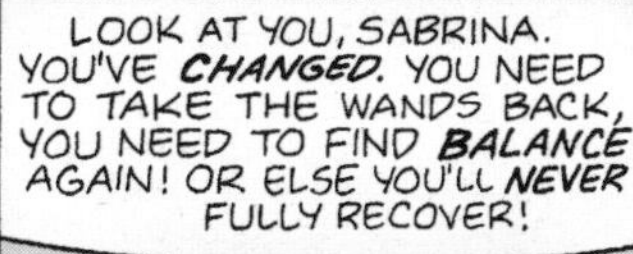
LOOK AT YOU, SABRINA. YOU'VE CHANGED. YOU NEED TO TAKE THE WANDS BACK, YOU NEED TO FIND BALANCE AGAIN! OR ELSE YOU'LL NEVER FULLY RECOVER!

THIS SHOULD DO THE TRICK!
WHAT DID YOU DO?
DUCT TAPE! I TOLD YOU IT FIXES EVERYTHING! THIS IS HOW WANDS SHOULD BE ANYWAY! POSITIVE AND NEGATIVE BALANCED AS ONE, LIKE A BATTERY!
SABRINA... IF I HAND THIS BACK TO YOU, CAN I TRUST YOU TO USE IT ONLY FOR GOOD?
I KNOW THE TEMPTATION MAY BE STRONG, BUT THE MORE YOU USE THE LIGHT END, THE BETTER YOU'LL FEEL...
YES... AND TO PROVE IT, I'LL UNDO THE ONE THING I SHOULD NEVER HAVE DONE...
LATER...

I'M INCREDIBLY SORRY I TREATED YOU SO HORRIBLY, AMY... I DON'T KNOW WHAT GOT INTO ME... WILL YOU GIVE ME ANOTHER CHANCE?
YOU REALLY HURT ME, HARVEY, SO I DON'T THINK I SHOULD... BUT, YES... I'LL GIVE YOU ONE MORE CHANCE...

I KNOW IT WAS HARD FOR YOU TO REPAIR THEIR RELATIONSHIP, SABRINA...
ESPECIALLY SINCE YOU STILL LOVE HARVEY... I'M PROUD OF YOU. DO YOU FEEL ANY BETTER?

A LITTLE. I THINK I HAVE A LONG WAY TO GO WITH THIS LIGHT WAND, THOUGH. I STILL FEEL ANGER INSIDE...
WHAT ARE YOU GOING TO DO?

IF I'M GOING TO USE THIS WAND FOR GOOD, I'M GOING TO LEARN TO RESTORE MEMORY-WIPES ONCE AND FOR ALL.
AND I'M GOING TO START WITH BATTY BARTHOLOMEW!
The End

NEXT, THE **SECRET HISTORY** OF SABRINA'S CAT **SALEM** IS REVEALED!

WHAT DID THIS **MASTER SORCERER-TURNED-FELINE** DO TO GET HIMSELF PERMANENTLY TRANSFORMED BY THE **MAGIC COUNCIL**?

Chapter 4

Salem's Secret PART 1
WRITER · TANIA DEL RIO ~ GUEST PENCILER · CHAD THOMAS
INKS · JIM AMASH ~ COLORS · JASON JENSEN ~ LETTERS · TERESA DAVIDSON
EDITOR/MANAGING EDITOR · MIKE PELLERITO ~ EDITOR-IN-CHIEF · VICTOR GORELICK
Ahh, IT'S NICE TO HAVE SABRINA BACK!
WE ALL KNEW THERE WAS SOMETHING WRONG WITH HER, BUT NO ONE KNEW WHY!
ACTUALLY... I KNEW WHY, OR AT LEAST I HAD A HUNCH.
I JUST DIDN'T RECOGNIZE THESE FOR WHAT THEY WERE AT FIRST... I THOUGHT THEY HAD BEEN DESTROYED LONG AGO...
ONCE, I WOULD HAVE GIVEN ANYTHING TO OWN THESE...

The Magic Realm, 1000 years ago...
The Batty Wizard
NO, NO, NO!
THIS ISN'T WHAT I WAS LOOKING FOR!
A-ARE YOU SURE?
Batty Wizard
OF COURSE I'M SURE! THERE'S NOT AN OUNCE OF MAGIC IN THIS THING! IT'S NOTHING MORE THAN A TWIG!
W-WITH ALL DUE RESPECT, SALEM, SIR... NO WANDS HAVE MAGIC IN THEM! IT'S THE USER THAT MAKES THEM MAGICAL!
YOU DON'T THINK I KNOW THIS?! WHAT DID I PAY YOU FOR EXACTLY?

Y-YOU P-PAID ME TO GET INFORMATION ON THE LOCATION OF A RARE TWO-SIDED DUALITY WAND.
THAT'S RIGHT.
AND DO YOU NOT REMEMBER ME TELLING YOU THAT THIS WAND IS NOT ACTUALLY A WAND, BUT AN EXTREMELY RARE UNICORN HORN? THAT'S WHY IT HAS MAGIC INSIDE!
AND I WANTED VALID INFORMATION ON ITS WHEREABOUTS, NOT SOME WORTHLESS STICK YOU FOUND IN A TRASH HEAP SOMEWHERE!
I-I-I'M S-SORRY!
I-I THOUGHT YOU WOULD BE MAD IF I CAME HERE EMPTY-HANDED! I COULDN'T FIND ANY INFORMATION ON YOUR UNICORN WAND. I DON'T EVEN THINK IT EXISTS! IT'S JUST A FAIRYTALE!
HOW DARE YOU WASTE MY TIME?! THIS IS MORE THAN JUST A FAIRYTALE!
FWOOSH

THIS JUST GOES TO SHOW THAT IF I WANT SOMETHING DONE, I HAVE TO DO IT MYSELF!
BUT IF I DO EVERYTHING MYSELF, TAKING OVER THE MAGIC REALM IS GOING TO TAKE FOREVER!
I NEED A TRUSTWORTHY ASSISTANT! I NEED MINIONS!
SWOOSH
I WON'T BE A MINION, BUT I MAY BE OF SOME ASSISTANCE!
WHO ARE YOU?!
YOU READ MY MIND!
THAT IS FORBIDDEN! IT'S OUT-LAWED!

FOR SOMEONE WHO WANTS TO TAKE OVER THE MAGIC REALM, YOU SURE SEEM WORRIED ABOUT RULES AND LAWS!
IN THIS CASE, I AM! VERY FEW PEOPLE CAN READ MINDS! IF I DO EVER BECOME LEADER OF THE REALM, ALL OF YOU WILL BE FOUND AND IMPRISONED!
VERY WELL. BUT INSTEAD OF FEARING ME, MAYBE YOU SHOULD THINK ABOUT HOW YOU COULD TAKE ADVANTAGE OF MY SKILLS!
GO ON...
MY NAME IS NOCTURNA. I'M THE CAPTAIN OF THE PIRATE VESSEL, SEASHIFTER.
I HAVE SEARCHED FOR AND FOUND MANY RARE TREASURES ON MY VOYAGES. I BELIEVE I CAN HELP YOU FIND THE WAND YOU SEEK.
AND WHAT DO YOU WANT IN RETURN?

I NEED A CAPABLE MAGIC USER TO JOIN MY RANKS AND HELP PROTECT US FROM ATTACK. ANYONE WHO SEEKS TO TAKE OVER THE REALM MUST SURELY BE ADEPT AT OFFENSIVE AND DEFENSIVE SPELLS!
WHAT ABOUT THE REST OF YOUR CREW?
THOSE LOUTS? THEY ONLY WORK FOR THE MONEY I PAY THEM.
THEY HAVE NO REAL LOYALTY TO ME AND EVEN LESS SKILL WITH MAGIC. I NEED SOMEONE POWERFUL ON MY SIDE!
WELL, I SUPPOSE IT COULDN'T HURT TO SEE MORE OF THE WORLD I PLAN TO CONQUER! VERY WELL, I'LL JOIN YOU UNDER ONE CONDITION.
YES?
STAY OUT OF MY MIND.
DEAL.

WELCOME ABOARD MY SHIP, SALEM!
BEFORE WE SET A COURSE, WHY DON'T YOU TELL ME MORE ABOUT THIS WAND YOU'RE LOOKING FOR?
I ASSUME YOU'VE HEARD THE FAIRYTALE ABOUT THE SPOILED UNICORN?
VAGUELY... BUT I GREW UP FAR FROM HERE.
ENLIGHTEN ME.
ONCE THERE WAS A UNICORN WHO, LIKE ALL UNICORNS, WAS VERY PURE AT HEART AND WHOSE HORN WAS FILLED WITH MAGIC.
LIKE ALL THE OTHERS, HE WOULD USE HIS MAGIC TO HELP THOSE IN NEED, AND HE ALWAYS BEHAVED WELL.

ONE DAY HE SPOTTED A SQUIRREL WHO HAD FALLEN INTO A STREAM.
NATURALLY, HE HURRIED TO SAVE HIS LIFE.
THE SQUIRREL WAS SO GRATEFUL THAT HE OFFERED THE UNICORN A GARLAND OF TASTY NUTS.
THE UNICORN THEN REALIZED THAT HIS GOOD DEEDS COULD BE REWARDED. FROM THEN ON, WHENEVER AN ANIMAL NEEDED HELP, THE UNICORN WOULD ASK FOR SOMETHING IN RETURN.
BEFORE LONG, THE UNICORN HAD MORE GIFTS THAN HE KNEW WHAT TO DO WITH. BUT HE STILL WASN'T SATISFIED.
BUT LITTLE DID THE UNICORN REALIZE, ALL HIS GREED WAS CAUSING HIS MAGIC HORN TO TURN BLACK WITH DECAY.

HIS MOTHER NOTICED THIS AND WARNED THE UNICORN THAT HE SHOULD NOT EXPECT ANYTHING FOR HIS GOOD DEEDS AND THAT IF HE HAD THE POWER TO HELP SOMEONE, HE SHOULD DO SO, WITHOUT QUESTION.
BUT NOW THAT THE UNICORN HAD RECEIVED SO MANY GIFTS...
...IT WAS TOO HARD FOR HIM TO GO BACK TO NOT EXPECTING ANY, AND HE CONTINUED TO ASK THE ANIMALS FOR A REWARD.
ONE DAY, THE UNICORN'S HORN FELL OFF...
...AND ALL HIS MAGIC WAS LOST!
HE WAS SOON MISTAKEN FOR A HORSE AND SPENT THE REST OF HIS DAYS SERVING OTHERS... WITH NO HOPE OF A REWARD IN RETURN.

AW, SUCH A SAD STORY.
NOW WHY WOULD YOU WANT THE HORN OF SUCH A POOR CREATURE AND WHAT GOOD WOULD IT DO YOU?

UNICORN HORNS ARE BEYOND RARE.
THEY ARE IMMORTAL CREATURES, SO IT IS IMPOSSIBLE TO KILL ONE FOR ITS HORN, WHICH CONTAINS AN AMAZING SUPPLY OF MAGIC... EVEN TAINTED, A FALLEN HORN WOULD MAKE AN AMAZING WAND.

VERY WELL. IF SUCH A HORN EXISTS, IT WOULD MOST LIKELY BE FOUND IN THE REGION WHERE UNICORNS ARE MOST COMMON! THE ISLAND OF THE ELVES!
HOWEVER, THEY ARE WELL PROTECTED AGAINST PIRATES THERE... ARE YOU UP FOR THE CHALLENGE?
I'VE NEVER BEEN MORE PREPARED!

THEN LET'S SET SAIL!

YOU NEVER TOLD ME THIS BOAT WAS SO UNSTABLE!
YOU'LL GET USED TO IT SOON ENOUGH!
BLEGGGH!!
I BETTER!
TROUBLE AHEAD!

10 O'CLOCK! A SEA SERPENT!
ALL THE WAY OUT HERE?
WAKE UP, SALEM! WE NEED YOU!
YOU BUNCH OF COWARDS! EVERY TIME TROUBLE COMES, YOU DISAPPEAR!
SORRY, M'LADY! NO AMOUNT OF MONEY IS WORTH THIS!
DON'T WORRY... IF WE COMBINE OUR MAGIC, WE SHOULD BE FINE.
WELL, THAT'S THE THING!
MY MIND-READING POWERS MAY BE STRONG, BUT THE REST OF MY MAGIC ABILITIES ARE WEAK! WHY DO YOU THINK I SAIL A SHIP INSTEAD OF JUST TELEPORTING?
GULP!
YOU'RE ON YOUR OWN!

RAAAGHH
YOU WANT TO CONQUER THE REALM! WHAT'S ONE LITTLE SEA SERPENT?
LITTLE?!

ZAP
HYAH!!!
THAT WAS EASY!
SALEM! BEHIND YOU!

UNGGH!
WHAP
ZAP
SLAM
WHOA, LOOK AT THAT JEWEL IN ITS CHEST, SALEM!
THAT MUST BE HIS CORE!

SALEM! DISTRACT HIM A MINUTE WHILE I GRAB IT!
NOCTURNA! NO!
COME... ON!
BLAASST
NOCTURNA!
SPLASH

WHOA! HE'S TWICE AS FAST IN THE WATER!
WOO! CLOSE ONE!
SWISH

ERGGH!
WHAP
ZAP
I'VE GOT TO HIT THE CORE!
ZAP

RAAAARGH!!
GGRRRGLE
MEDIC!
IS THERE A MEDIC ON THIS SHIP?

YOU'RE ALL *WORTHLESS* LUMPS! I'D THROW YOU *OVERBOARD* IF I WERE CAPTAIN!

COUGH
COUGH
SALEM...
THANK YOU.
I-I WOULDN'T HAVE DONE IT, BUT YOUR CREW WAS WORTHLESS!
DID YOU GET THE GEM?
WHAT?
THE SERPENT'S GEM! WHERE IS IT?
IT SANK...
I WAS TOO BUSY SAVING YOU!

WHAT?! DO YOU HAVE ANY IDEA WHAT THE GEM MUST BE WORTH? IT'S WORTH MORE THAN ME!
IF YOU DIED, IT WOULDN'T MATTER!
NOOOOOO! LET ME GO!
WELL, I'M ALIVE NOW! I MUST HAVE IT!!!
DIDN'T YOU LEARN ANYTHING FROM THE UNICORN STORY?!
To be continued...

S **SALEM**'S JOURNEY CONTINUES,
EW SURPRISES AND CHALLENGES LIE
HEAD OF HIM AND HIS NEWFOUND
RTNER, **NOCTURNA**.

LL THEY FIND THE **UNICORN HORN**
EY SEEK?

ID WHAT'S MORE, HOW WILL SALEM
SE ITS **AWESOME POWER**?

Chapter 5

Salem's Secret PART 2
WRITER · TANIA DEL RIO
PENCILS · CHAD THOMAS
INKS · JIM AMASH
COLORS · JASON JENSEN
LETTERS · TERESA DAVIDSON
EDITOR/MANAGING EDITOR
MIKE PELLERITO
EDITOR-IN-CHIEF · VICTOR GORELICK
SALEM, LOOK! THERE IT IS! THE ISLAND OF THE ELVES, HOME OF THE MOST MAGICAL, MOST PEACEFUL PEOPLE IN THE REALM!
AND HOME TO THE MOST ELUSIVE CREATURES IN THE REALM-- UNICORNS! IF I'M GOING TO FIND THAT FALLEN UNICORN HORN, WHAT BETTER PLACE TO LOOK THAN HERE?
AS IF YOU NEEDED ANY MORE POWER!
YOU SINGLE-HANDEDLY SAVED THIS SHIP FROM A SEA MONSTER ATTACK!*
Meh-- THAT'S NOTHING COMPARED TO TAKING OVER THE ENTIRE REALM!
AND WITH THAT UNICORN WAND IN MY POSSESSION, I'LL BE UNSTOPPABLE!
* LAST CHAPTER

WHOA!
BLAST
WHAT'S GOING ON?!
SORRY, CAP'N! I FELL ASLEEP!
GET OUT OF OUR WATERS, OR WE'LL BLAST YOUR SHIP!
IT'S A FREE REALM! I'LL GO WHERE I PLEASE!
WE DON'T ALLOW PIRATES ON OUR ISLAND. NOW BACK OFF OR PAY THE PRICE!
ZAP

I THOUGHT YOU SAID ELVES WERE THE MOST PEACEFUL--
WHOA!
NOW, JUST A MINUTE! ARE YOU ACCUSING A LADY SUCH AS MYSELF OF BEING A PIRATE? THIS IS JUST A BIG MISUNDERSTANDING!
OH, REALLY? TRY TELLING THAT TO YOUR CREW.
♪OOOOOOH...
♪ I'LL SING ME A PIRATE SHANTY! LIVIN' LIFE ON THE HIGH SEAS! PILLAGING AND STEALING MONEY! YES, I LOVE BEIN' PIRATE-Y! ♪

SNAP
FIRE!
ZAP
ZAP
ZAP
SALEM! DO SOMETHING!
MY PLEASURE!
ZAP

IT'S NO USE!
BLAST
BLAST

YOU'RE *OUTNUMBERED* AND THEIR MAGIC IS *TOO* STRONG! THEY'RE DESTROYING MY SHIP!
STAY BACK! I CAN *HANDLE* THIS!
RETREAT! TURN THIS SHIP AROUND!

NOCTURNA, *WHY* ARE WE *FLEEING?* I HAVE IT UNDER CONTROL!
DON'T *QUESTION* MY DECISIONS! I'M THE CAPTAIN OF THIS SHIP AND WE'VE ALREADY TAKEN TOO MUCH DAMAGE!

I CAN REPAIR THE DAMAGE MAGICALLY!
NOW, TURN BACK!
NO, MAGIC IS ONLY A TEMPORARY SOLUTION. BESIDES, SAVE YOUR STRENGTH...
YOU'LL NEED IT FOR TELEPORTING ONTO THE ISLAND! I'LL MEET YOU THERE! WE'LL JUST ANCHOR THE SHIP HERE AND LET THE CREW WAIT FOR OUR RETURN!
WELL, IT WAS A LOT EASIER TO SNEAK ONTO THE ISLAND, JUST THE TWO OF US...
FWIP FWIP FWIP FWIP FWIP FWIP
BUT WHAT HAPPENS IF YOU STUMBLE ACROSS AN ELVIN TREASURE TROVE?
HOW DO YOU PLAN TO GET EVERYTHING BACK TO YOUR SHIP WITHOUT BEING SEEN?

WELL, I FIGURE I'M HERE FOR ONE REASON, AND THAT'S TO HELP YOU FIND THIS UNICORN WAND. I ALREADY HAVE ENOUGH TREASURE AS IT IS...
WHAT?!
YOU'RE A PIRATE, REMEMBER? WHY ARE YOU SO INTERESTED IN HELPING ME OUT, ANYWAY?
HEY, I'M JUST HOLDING UP MY END OF THE BARGAIN. YOU AGREED TO JOIN MY CREW AS A MAGIC USER...
AND IN RETURN I SAID I'D HELP YOU FIND THIS WAND YOU SEEK...
AND BESIDES...
YOU SAVED MY LIFE!
RIGHT...
WELL, WE BETTER START LOOKING, eh?

LET'S ASK AROUND THERE AND SEE IF WE CAN LEARN WHERE THE UNICORNS LIVE.
VERY WELL, BUT IT WON'T BE THAT EASY. ELVES ARE VERY SECRETIVE PEOPLE...
Er, EXCUSE ME, SIR. WE'RE SIMPLE TOURISTS VISITING YOUR LOVELY ISLAND AND WERE HOPING YOU COULD TELL US WHERE WE CAN FIND UNICORNS.
WHY SUUUURE!
WANT ME TO DRAW YOU A MAP?
POOF
WELL, THAT WAS EASY!
HEH HEH HEH

HERE WE ARE!
I DON'T SEE ANY UNICORNS, THOUGH...
OOF!
SLAM!
AN INVISIBILITY SHIELD!
IT MUST BE LIKE A GIANT DOME PROTECTING THE AREA.

NOTHING A LITTLE MAGIC CAN'T BREAK THROUGH!
ZAP

ERGH!
BLAST
THE DOME IS COVERED IN ELVISH WRITING!
UGH! THAT MEANS, ONLY AN ELF'S MAGIC CAN BREAK THROUGH THE BARRIER...
THAT OLD ELF WAS JUST FOOLING WITH US WHEN HE GAVE US THAT MAP!
I DOUBT A SINGLE ELF IS GOING TO BE WILLING TO HELP US BREAK THROUGH THE DOME! LIKE I SAID, THEY'RE DIFFICULT!
NOCTURNA, YOU SHOULD KNOW THAT EVERY PERSON-- EVEN ELVES--HAVE A PRICE!
WE'LL JUST GO TO THE TAVERN IN TOWN AND PAY SOMEONE TO HELP US!

NO WAY.
I PAY VERY WELL...
DON'T MATTER.
TOURISTS HAVE NO BUSINESS IN UNICORN GROUNDS... THAT'S SACRED TERRITORY, THERE.
THERE'S PLENTY OF OTHER STUFF TO SEE ON THIS ISLAND...
NOW, MOVE ALONG.
SALEM! IT'S THE ELVES FROM EARLIER. WE SHOULD GET OUT OF HERE BEFORE THEY SEE US!
GREAT. NOW WHAT?
I TOLD YOU IT WOULDN'T BE EASY!
I WISH THERE WAS AN ELF ON MY CREW...
NOT THAT MY CREW IS OF MUCH HELP ANYWAY...

SALEM?
WHAT IS IT?

SALEM... SHE'S JUST A *CHILD*.
AND AN *ORPHAN* AT THAT!

EVEN *BETTER*!
BESIDES, SHE LOOKS LIKE SHE COULD USE SOME EXTRA *CASH*. EVERYONE HAS A PRICE, *EVEN* CHILDREN!

HEY THERE, LITTLE GIRL! YOUR MAGIC IS VERY *IMPRESSIVE*! WHAT'S YOUR NAME?
S-SELES.

HERE YOU GO, SELES! THIS IS FOR YOU!
REALLY?!

SURE! AND I HAVE LOTS MORE, TOO! HAVE YOU SEEN A REAL-LIFE UNICORN?
OH, I PLAY WITH THE UNICORNS ALL THE TIME!
THEY'RE MY FRIENDS!

IS THAT RIGHT? HOW EXCITING!

IT STILL SEEMS WRONG... SHE'S TOO YOUNG TO KNOW WHAT'S GOING ON!

WE'RE USING HER!

OF COURSE WE'RE USING HER! BUT ONLY FOR A LITTLE WHILE, AND WE'LL PAY HER WELL! BESIDES, IF SHE CAN LEAD US TO UNICORNS, I BET SHE CAN LEAD US TO OTHER SECRET TREASURES, TOO! YOU ARE A PIRATE, RIGHT?

OF COURSE! THAT DOESN'T MEAN I DON'T HAVE MORALS! BUT...
I GUESS WE CAN KEEP HER AROUND FOR A LITTLE WHILE AND SEE WHAT HAPPENS!

HERE WE ARE!
CAN YOU OPEN THE WAY FOR US, SELES? WE NEED YOUR HELP TO SEE THE UNICORNS!
COME ON!
THIS WAY!

HI, GUYS! I BROUGHT SOME NEW FRIENDS!
WHAT'S WRONG? WHY ARE YOU GOING AWAY? WHY ARE YOU UPSET?
THE UNICORNS DON'T TRUST HER ANYMORE FOR BRINGING US HERE.
WE'VE PROBABLY JUST CAUSED HER TO LOSE THE ONLY FRIENDS SHE'S EVER HAD!
Eh, SHE'S YOUNG. SHE'LL MAKE MORE FRIENDS.
I DON'T KNOW WHY THE UNICORNS ARE BEING THIS WAY! THEY USUALLY LIKE TO PLAY WITH ME!
AW...
HEY! WHAT'S THAT?

A GRAVE? BUT UNICORNS ARE IMMORTAL!
THE UNICORNS TOLD ME THIS GRAVE IS A WARNING TO THEM.
"EVEN IMMORTAL CREATURES CAN FALL TO GREED"

THIS IS IT! I KNEW IT!
WAIT, SALEM! YOU CAN'T TAKE THAT FROM THE GRAVE! IT'S JUST WRONG!
BUT THIS IS THE WHOLE REASON WE CAME!
WHAT DOES IT MATTER IF IT'S EMBEDDED IN SOME ROCK?
IT'S NOT JUST A ROCK! IT'S A TOMBSTONE!
AND IF YOU STEAL FROM IT, YOU'RE NO BETTER THAN A GRAVE ROBBER! IT'S DISRESPECTFUL!
AND YOU CALL YOURSELF A PIRATE! COME ON, NOCTURNA! THE UNICORN IS LONG GONE! I BET HE'D LOVE FOR HIS HORN TO BE USED AGAIN!
PLEASE, MR. SALEM! DON'T DO IT!

SORRY, KID.
YES! YES!! IT'S MINE AT LAST!
WHAT POWER!
WHAT INCREDIBLE MAGIC!
I CAN DO ANYTHING NOW!
AND WHEN I TAKE OVER THE WORLD, I WANT YOU TO BE RIGHT BESIDE ME!

NOW LET'S GET OUT OF HERE BEFORE THE UNICORNS CHANGE THEIR PEACEFUL WAYS AND TRY TO CHALLENGE US!
WAIT! WHAT ABOUT SELES?
I ALREADY PAID HER, DON'T WORRY.
NO, SHE'S COMING WITH US!
THE UNICORNS WILL NEVER FORGIVE HER FOR BRINGING US HERE! THE LEAST WE CAN DO IS TAKE HER IN!
FINE, WHATEVER. I HAVE THE WAND AND THAT'S ALL THAT MATTERS!

THEY'RE LIKE THE FAMILY I'VE NEVER HAD...
HE WANTS ME TO BE BY HIS SIDE!
HE LOVES ME!
OR... DOES HE?
SORRY, SALEM. I KNOW I PROMISED NOT TO READ YOUR MIND... BUT I HAVE TO KNOW!
FZZT

ALL HIS THOUGHTS ARE OF **POWER** AND **DESTRUCTION** AND **WAR**! I HAD NO IDEA! HOW **HORRIBLE**!

AND... HE DOESN'T THINK OF ME **AT ALL**!

HE WAS JUST **USING** ME... JUST LIKE HE USED SELES...
HE DOESN'T CARE ABOUT ANYONE BUT **HIMSELF**... AND **TAKING OVER** THE REALM.

I **CAN'T** LET HIM DO THAT!

Mrrgh... mm...
I FELL FOR HIM, AND I HELPED HIM DO SOMETHING HORRIBLE--ROB A UNICORN'S GRAVE! WHAT GOT INTO ME?! AM I THAT BLINDED BY LOVE?
AT LEAST I CAN RIGHT THIS WRONG.
FZZZZT
KRAK!
GASP!
NOCTURNA! WHAT ARE YOU DOING?
I CAN'T HELP YOU DO THIS ANYMORE, SALEM! IT'S WRONG!

HOW DARE YOU?! YOU'LL REGRET THIS!
YOU'RE RIGHT! I DO REGRET THIS! I REGRET THAT YOU AREN'T THE PERSON I THOUGHT YOU WERE!
YOU'LL PAY FOR THIS!
BET YOU WISH YOU WERE ADEPT AT MAGIC NOW, huh?
WAAAH!!

NOW THAT **SALEM'S** TALE IS TOLD, WE RETURN TO THE PRESENT DAY, WHERE **SABRINA** AND **LLANDRA** ATTEMPT TO RESTORE THE MEMORIES OF THE **ORIGINAL FOUR BLADES**!

WILL THEIR PLAN **WORK**?

PERHAPS **NOT** IN THE WAY THAT YOU THINK!

Chapter 6

REMEMBRANCE PART 1

WRITER & PENCILER · TANIA DEL RIO ~ INKS · JIM AMASH
COLORS · JASON JENSEN ~ LETTERS · TERESA DAVIDSON
EDITOR/MANAGING EDITOR · MIKE PELLERITO
EDITOR-IN-CHIEF · VICTOR GORELICK

WHEN I FOUND THIS WAND, IT WAS IN TWO PIECES. I THOUGHT IT WAS JUST A COOL RELIC FROM THE PAST-- A HARMLESS ANTIQUE.
I DIDN'T REALIZE THAT BY USING THE DARK WAND MORE THAN THE LIGHT WAND, I WAS CORRUPTING MY SOUL... I DID SOME HORRIBLE THINGS.
I WISH I COULD JUST THROW THIS AWAY AND NEVER SEE IT AGAIN...
BUT THE ONLY WAY I'LL EVER RETURN TO NORMAL IS IF I USE THE LIGHT, RESTORATIVE END OF THIS WAND ENOUGH TIMES TO BALANCE OUT THE DARKNESS I CREATED BEFORE...

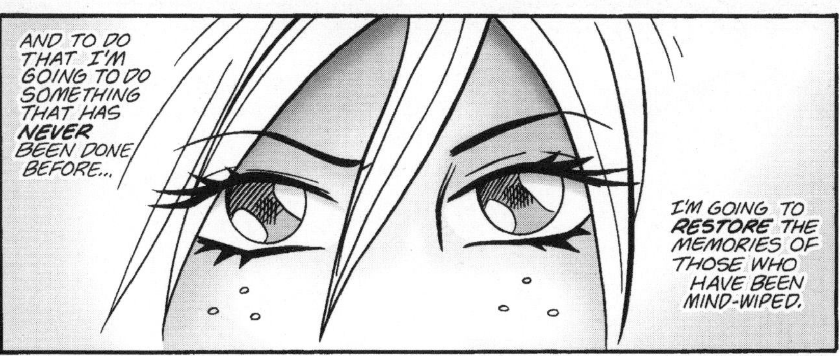
AND TO DO THAT I'M GOING TO DO SOMETHING THAT HAS NEVER BEEN DONE BEFORE...
I'M GOING TO RESTORE THE MEMORIES OF THOSE WHO HAVE BEEN MIND-WIPED.

STARTING WITH MY TUTOR, BATTY BARTHOLOMEW!

ARE YOU SURE HE'S GOING TO MEET US HERE LIKE HE SAID?
IS HE REALLY OKAY WITH BEING YOUR GUINEA PIG?
THIS ISN'T SOME KIND OF TEST, LLANDRA. IT'S GONNA WORK. I JUST KNOW IT!

IF YOU BELIEVE IN THAT WAND SO MUCH, WHY DON'T YOU WANT TO USE IT IN THE MAGICAL FOREST, WHERE BATTY LIVES?
MOST SPELLS WON'T WORK THERE-- BUT YOUR WAND DOES!
WELL, YOU'RE RIGHT.
I GUESS PART OF ME IS AFRAID SOMETHING MIGHT GO WRONG. NOT THE SPELL ITSELF...
BUT ME.
THE DARKNESS ISN'T OUT OF MY SYSTEM YET... I NEED YOU HERE IN CASE IT TAKES HOLD OF ME AGAIN. AND IF THINGS GO REALLY BAD, WELL, THERE ARE PROFESSORS NEARBY...

I DON'T THINK THAT'S GOING TO HAPPEN, SABRINA.
YOU'VE GOTTEN THROUGH THE WORST OF IT. I BELIEVE YOU CAN OVERCOME IT ONCE AND FOR ALL!
THANKS...
I'M NOT LATE FOR MY FIRST DAY OF SCHOOL, AM I?
HUFF
PUFF

WHAT? YOU'RE NOT GOING TO SCHOOL, BATTY. WE JUST ASKED YOU TO MEET US HERE.
BUT I ALREADY DID THE HOMEWORK! A REPORT AND A TAKE-HOME QUIZ! I THINK I DID GOOD, TOO!
WELL, EXCEPT FOR PROBLEM 9. THAT WAS A TOUGHIE!
QUIZ
1
2
3

BATTY, I ASKED YOU TO COME HERE SO I CAN TRY AND RESTORE YOUR MEMORY... REMEMBER?
Um... NO?
CASE IN POINT.
I'VE LEARNED THAT YOU USED TO BE A MEMBER OF THE ORIGINAL FOUR BLADES MOVEMENT.
IF I CAN RESTORE YOUR MEMORY, MAYBE YOU CAN TELL US EVERYTHING YOU KNOW ABOUT IT! MAYBE YOU CAN JOIN OUR NEW CAUSE!
AND YOU MIGHT FEEL LESS SCATTERBRAINED TOO!
WELL, SURE!
FIRE AWAY!

PLEASE WORK...
TREMBLE TREMBLE

ZAP
WHAT DID I DO?!
AAAHHH!!
AAAAHAHAHAHAHAHAHA!
THAT TICKLES!
PHEW!

DID IT WORK?
DO YOU... REMEMBER?

I...
I...
REMEMBER!

YOU DO?!!
YES! I REMEMBER!
I REMEMBER!
I REMEMBER!

YOU REMEMBER! LLANDRA, HE REMEMBERS!
YOU DID IT, SABRINA! YOU DID THE IMPOSSIBLE!
BATTY! WHAT DO YOU REMEMBER? TELL US!
I REMEMBER...

I REMEMBER THE ANSWER TO PROBLEM 9! WOOO!
QUIZ
1.
2.
3.

NOW I'M SURE TO GET A PERFECT SCORE!
QUIZ
WAIT! IS THAT ALL? DON'T YOU REMEMBER ANYTHING ELSE? YOUR PAST? YOUR HISTORY?
OF COURSE!
BUT I'LL BE HISTORY IF I DON'T GET TO CLASS ON TIME! PICK ME UP AT 3:30! BUT STAY IN THE CAR. I DON'T WANT YOU TO EMBARRASS ME IN FRONT OF MY FRIENDS!

DID... DID IT WORK OR NOT?
I'M NOT SURE. EITHER WAY, HE'S STILL AS BATTY AS EVER...

WHO AM I FOOLING?
WHAT MADE ME THINK I COULD BRING BACK SOMETHING THAT WAS ERASED? HE'S NO DIFFERENT THAN BEFORE! HE DOESN'T REMEMBER ANYTHING!

AND LOOK! YOUR HANDS HAVE RETURNED TO NORMAL! THAT MUST BE A SIGN YOUR SPELL WORKED!
I DUNNO, SABRINA... HE MIGHT JUST BE PLAYING DUMB.
I DUNNO... THERE'S ONLY ONE WAY TO KNOW FOR SURE... AND THAT'S TO RESTORE THE MEMORY OF SOMEONE ELSE.
THERE ARE LOTS OF EX-FOUR BLADES OUT THERE. SHINJI HAS A LIST, RIGHT?

SABRINA! WHAT ABOUT HARVEY?
YOU COULD RESTORE HIS MEMORY! MAKE HIM REMEMBER YOU AND WHAT YOU MEANT TO HIM!
YOU THINK I HAVEN'T THOUGHT OF THAT? I CAN'T DO IT!
I MEAN, I COULD... BUT I SHOULDN'T...
IT WOULD BE FOR A PURELY SELFISH REASON... AND THAT WOULDN'T HELP ME GET RID OF THIS DARKNESS INSIDE...

YOU'RE RIGHT. I SHOULDN'T HAVE MENTIONED IT. BUT MAYBE ONE DAY YOU'LL BE BALANCED ENOUGH TO DO IT, SABRINA. DON'T GIVE UP HOPE.
SNIFF

HEY, LET'S GO FIND SHINJI AND GET THIS LIST OF NAMES HE HAS! THAT'S A START!

NO WAY.

I DON'T TRUST SABRINA ANYMORE. SHE LOST THE MANA LEAF I ENTRUSTED HER WITH!
I DIDN'T LOSE IT! HEMLOCK STOLE IT!

SWOOSH
PROVE IT!

GRR! YOU WERE EAVESDROPPING ON US!
POOF
SHE'S MY GIRLFRIEND, SABRINA! I KNEW SHE WAS HERE ALL ALONG!
YOU KNOW, HER ABILITY TO TURN INTO A BAT COMES IN QUITE HANDY ON MISSIONS.
YEAH, IT ALLOWS HER TO SNEAK INTO MY HOUSE AND STEAL MY MANA LEAF!
STOP TRYING TO BLAME ME FOR YOUR MISTAKES, SABRINA. IT'S GETTING OLD.
LISTEN, THE POINT IS, WE ORIGINALLY GOT THE DYING LEAF TO PROVE THAT THE QUEEN IS ALLOWING THE MAGIC REALM TO DIE. IT'S GONE, SO WE NEED TO THINK OF ANOTHER WAY TO PROVE TO THE PEOPLE THAT OUR CAUSE IS JUST!

AND THE SOLUTION LIES WITH SABRINA!
SHE HAS THE ABILITY TO RESTORE MEMORY! IF WE CAN MAKE THE EX-FOUR BLADES REMEMBER THEIR PASTS, THEY WILL BE WALKING PROOF THAT THE MAGIC COUNCIL IS TRYING TO HIDE SOMETHING!
PLUS, THEY'LL BE SURE TO JOIN OUR CAUSE AND STRENGTHEN OUR NUMBERS! IT'S THE BEST THING WE HAVE GOING FOR US RIGHT NOW!

IT'S NOT SABRINA THAT HAS THIS ABILITY, IT'S THAT WAND. LET ME TAKE IT AND I'LL DO THE RESTORING!
NO!
OW!
SABRINA! YOU HAVE TO STOP USING THE DARK END OF THE WAND! YOU'LL NEVER HEAL AT THIS RATE!
I-I'M SORRY. IT'S HARD TO CONTROL SOMETIMES.
HEH HEH HEH...
IS IT WEIRD THAT I ACTUALLY LIKE SABRINA BETTER THIS WAY?
Um... YEAH.

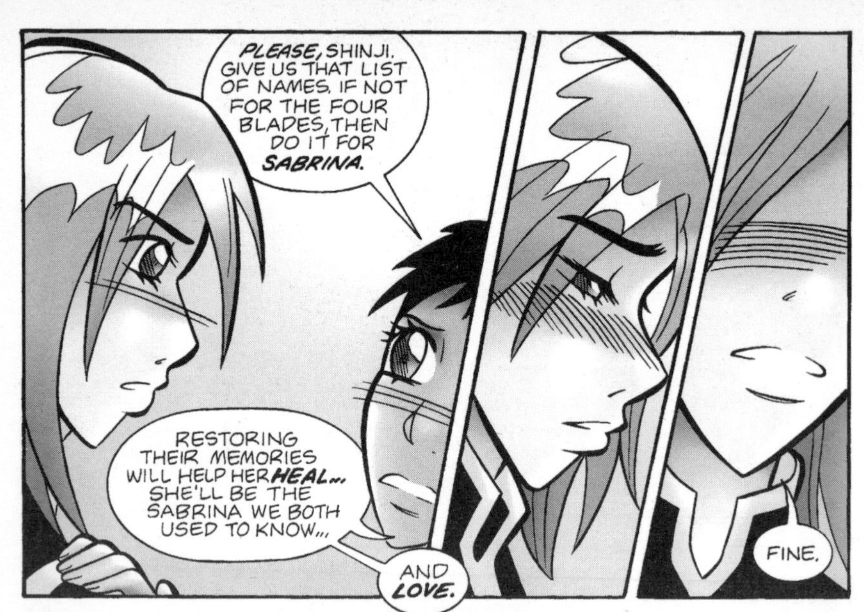
PLEASE, SHINJI. GIVE US THAT LIST OF NAMES. IF NOT FOR THE FOUR BLADES, THEN DO IT FOR SABRINA.
RESTORING THEIR MEMORIES WILL HELP HER HEAL... SHE'LL BE THE SABRINA WE BOTH USED TO KNOW...
AND LOVE.
FINE.

SO HOW SHOULD WE GO ABOUT THIS? JUST SHOW UP AT THEIR DOORS AND ZAP THEM?
I THINK IT MIGHT BE BEST IF WE TRY TO EXPLAIN WHAT WE'RE DOING. WE DON'T WANT TO FREAK PEOPLE OUT!
LOOK, THERE'S A COUPLE OF PEOPLE WHO LIVE OVER IN THE MISTY MARSHES. LET'S GO THERE FIRST.

WELL, HERE GOES NOTHING...
KNOCK
KNOCK
HELLO?
Uh... HELLO! THIS MAY SOUND STRANGE, BUT I'M HERE TO RESTORE YOUR MEMORY.
WHAT? MY MEMORY IS JUST FINE! IS THIS SOME KIND OF JOKE? A HIDDEN CAMERA THING?
NO, THIS IS FOR REAL! TELL ME, WHAT DO YOU REMEMBER OF FOUR BLADES DAY?
IT'S A YEARLY CELEBRATION... FIREWORKS... COSTUMES... FAIRS...
BUT WHAT DO YOU REMEMBER OF YOUR INVOLVEMENT IN THE ORIGINAL FOUR BLADES DAY?

WHAT ARE YOU ACCUSING ME OF?
HOW DARE YOU COME TO MY DOOR LIKE THIS AND INTERROGATE ME?!
WE'RE JUST TRYING TO HELP! NOW IF YOU JUST LET ME--
DON'T POINT THAT THING AT ME!
WHAT'S WRONG WITH YOU? I'M CALLING THE MAGI-SECURITY!
SLAM!
LET'S GET OUT OF HERE!
THIS IS GONNA BE HARDER THAN I THOUGHT!
ANOTHER EX-BLADE LIVES IN THIS AREA. MAYBE WE SHOULD TRY AGAIN... MAYBE THE NEXT PERSON WILL BE MORE WILLING TO LISTEN!
NO ONE'S GOING TO LIKE HAVING A WAND POINTED AT THEM. I SAY WE SKIP THE SMALL TALK AND JUST AMBUSH THEM!

HEY! THAT'S SHINJI'S OLDER BROTHER! WHAT'S HE DOING HERE?
KENICHI! HEY!
UMPH!

WHAT ARE YOU DOING?! KENICHI WORKS FOR MAGI-SECURITY!
HE'S PROBABLY RESPONDING TO THAT LADY'S CALL! IF HE FINDS OUT WE'RE THE CULPRITS, WE'RE GOING TO HAVE A TOUGH TIME EXPLAINING THINGS!
OOPS...
YOU'RE RIGHT. MAYBE WE SHOULD SKIP THE EXPLANATIONS AND JUST ZAP PEOPLE AS DISCREETLY AS POSSIBLE. WE'LL ASK QUESTIONS LATER.
RIGHT! IN FACT, ONCE THEIR MEMORIES HAVE BEEN RESTORED, IF WE CAN GET THEM ALL IN ONE PLACE AT THE SAME TIME, WE CAN CONVINCE THEM TO JOIN THE NEW FOUR BLADES AS A GROUP!
GOOD IDEA!
LET'S DO THIS!

eh?
ZAP
ZAP
ZAP
MEETING
MOON-DAY

HOW ARE YOU FEELING, SABRINA? YOU'RE FINALLY LOOKING NORMAL AGAIN!
I FEEL GREAT! ALL THIS RESTORATIVE MAGIC IS JUST WHAT I NEEDED!
I JUST HOPE THESE PEOPLE ACTUALLY SHOW UP TO THE FOUR BLADES MEETING.
ME TOO.
YOU INVITED THEM ALL HERE?! TO OUR SECRET HEADQUARTERS?! WHAT IF YOUR CALLING CARDS FALL INTO THE WRONG HANDS?
SHINJI, I KNOW IT WAS RISKY... BUT THIS WAS THE BEST WAY TO GET ALL OF THEM HERE ALL AT ONCE!
AND WHAT IF NO ONE SHOWS UP? WHAT IF YOUR MEMORY SPELL DIDN'T WORK? SOMEONE COULD TURN US IN!
THERE'S A BUNCH OF PEOPLE OUTSIDE... THEY'RE ASKING ABOUT THE FOUR BLADES MEETING.
HI-5!
IT WORKED!

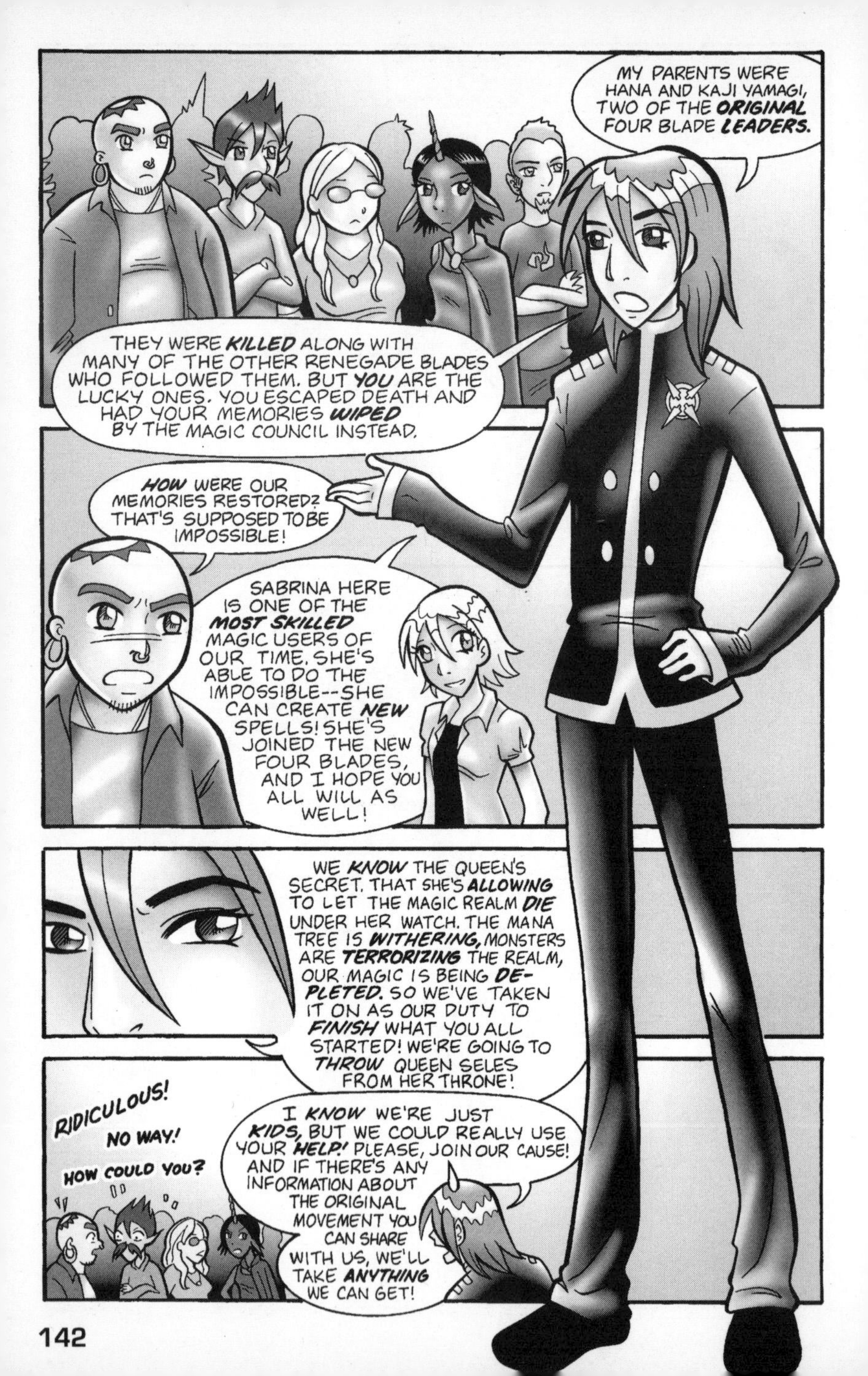
MY PARENTS WERE HANA AND KAJI YAMAGI, TWO OF THE ORIGINAL FOUR BLADE LEADERS.
THEY WERE KILLED ALONG WITH MANY OF THE OTHER RENEGADE BLADES WHO FOLLOWED THEM. BUT YOU ARE THE LUCKY ONES. YOU ESCAPED DEATH AND HAD YOUR MEMORIES WIPED BY THE MAGIC COUNCIL INSTEAD.
HOW WERE OUR MEMORIES RESTORED? THAT'S SUPPOSED TO BE IMPOSSIBLE!
SABRINA HERE IS ONE OF THE MOST SKILLED MAGIC USERS OF OUR TIME. SHE'S ABLE TO DO THE IMPOSSIBLE--SHE CAN CREATE NEW SPELLS! SHE'S JOINED THE NEW FOUR BLADES, AND I HOPE YOU ALL WILL AS WELL!
WE KNOW THE QUEEN'S SECRET. THAT SHE'S ALLOWING TO LET THE MAGIC REALM DIE UNDER HER WATCH. THE MANA TREE IS WITHERING, MONSTERS ARE TERRORIZING THE REALM, OUR MAGIC IS BEING DE-PLETED. SO WE'VE TAKEN IT ON AS OUR DUTY TO FINISH WHAT YOU ALL STARTED! WE'RE GOING TO THROW QUEEN SELES FROM HER THRONE!
RIDICULOUS!
NO WAY!
HOW COULD YOU?
I KNOW WE'RE JUST KIDS, BUT WE COULD REALLY USE YOUR HELP! PLEASE, JOIN OUR CAUSE! AND IF THERE'S ANY INFORMATION ABOUT THE ORIGINAL MOVEMENT YOU CAN SHARE WITH US, WE'LL TAKE ANYTHING WE CAN GET!

I'M AFRAID THAT WON'T BE POSSIBLE!

COMMANDER BARTHOLOMEW!
AN HONOR TO SEE YOU AGAIN!
BOW
YOU'RE ALIVE!
I THOUGHT YOU WERE CAPTURED AT THAT FINAL BATTLE!

WHY CAN'T YOU HELP US, SIR?
BECAUSE WE ORIGINAL RENEGADE BLADES SWORE AN OATH. TO PROTECT THE QUEEN, NOT OVER-THROW HER.
WHAT?!
I DON'T UNDERSTAND! WHAT DO YOU MEAN?

I CAN'T TELL YOU, BECAUSE WE ALSO SWORE AN OATH OF SECRECY.
ALL I CAN TELL YOU IS THAT IF YOU CONTINUE THIS HARE-BRAINED PLAN TO THROW SELES FROM HER THRONE, YOU'LL HAVE TO GET THROUGH US FIRST!
IS THAT A THREAT?!
WE RESTORE YOUR MEMORY AND THIS IS THE THANKS WE GET?
SHINJI, WAIT!
HE DOESN'T KNOW WHAT HE'S TALKING ABOUT! HE'S STILL BATTY!
THAT'S NOT A VERY NICE THING TO SAY ABOUT YOUR MENTOR!
AND ON TOP OF THAT, YOU FORGOT TO PICK ME UP FROM SCHOOL!
ORIGINAL BLADES, FOLLOW ME. WE HAVE SOME CATCHING UP TO DO!

THE ORIGINAL **RENEGADE BLADES** HAVE HAD THEIR MEMORIES RESTORED, BUT IS THAT SUCH A GOOD THING?

LOOKS LIKE THE **FOUR BLADES** HAVE THEIR WORK **"CUT"** OUT FOR THEM!

Chapter 7

Remembrance part 2
WRITER · TANIA DEL RIO
PENCILS · LINDSAY CIBOS
INKS · JIM AMASH
COLORS · JASON JENSEN
LETTERS · TERESA DAVIDSON
EDITOR/MANAGING EDITOR
MIKE PELLERITO
EDITOR-IN-CHIEF
VICTOR GORELICK
"MONSTERS HAVE BEEN BECOMING MORE FREQUENT IN THE FORESTS AND PLAINS...

"AND WHAT'S WORSE, THEY'RE BEGINNING TO VENTURE INTO POPULATED AREAS.
AAAAAHH!!
"THERE HAVE BEEN 5 MORE ATTACKS THIS WEEK, ALONE!"

AS THE CZARINA OF DECREE, I THINK MEASURES MUST BE TAKEN TO PROTECT OUR CITIZENS!

MEASURES HAVE BEEN TAKEN!
AS THE CZARINA OF DEFENSE, I'VE ASSEMBLED HUNTING PARTIES TO PATROL THE WILDERNESS AND ERADICATE THE MONSTERS!

IT'S NOT ENOUGH! THE BEASTS ARE BECOMING BOLDER AND THEIR NUMBERS ARE GROWING! IT'S NO LONGER SAFE TO BE OUTSIDE AFTER DARK!
AND IN A REALM WHERE THERE ARE MORE DARK HOURS THAN LIGHT, WHAT DO YOU PROPOSE, GALIENA? SOME KIND OF CURFEW?!

PRECISELY!
RIDICULOUS!
NO WAY!
HA!

THIS IS NOT JUST FOR THE CITIZENS' SAFETY, BUT FOR OUR QUEEN'S!
THE FOURBLADES ARE BACK AND YOU ALL KNOW WHAT THAT MEANS! A CURFEW WOULD PREVENT THEM FROM MEETING AFTER-HOURS!

QUEEN SELES, THIS IS YOUR DECISION. WILL YOU ENACT A CURFEW TO PROTECT OUR PEOPLE-- AND YOURSELF?

WAIT! WHAT ABOUT ALL THE CHARM SCHOOLS? THEY TAKE PLACE AT NIGHT... ARE YOU SUGGESTING WE SHUT THOSE DOWN AS WELL?

WHATEVER IT TAKES!

SO WHAT WILL IT BE, YOUR HIGHNESS? WILL YOU TAKE THE STEPS NECESSARY TO PROTECT YOUR PEOPLE? IT IS YOUR JOB, AFTER ALL!

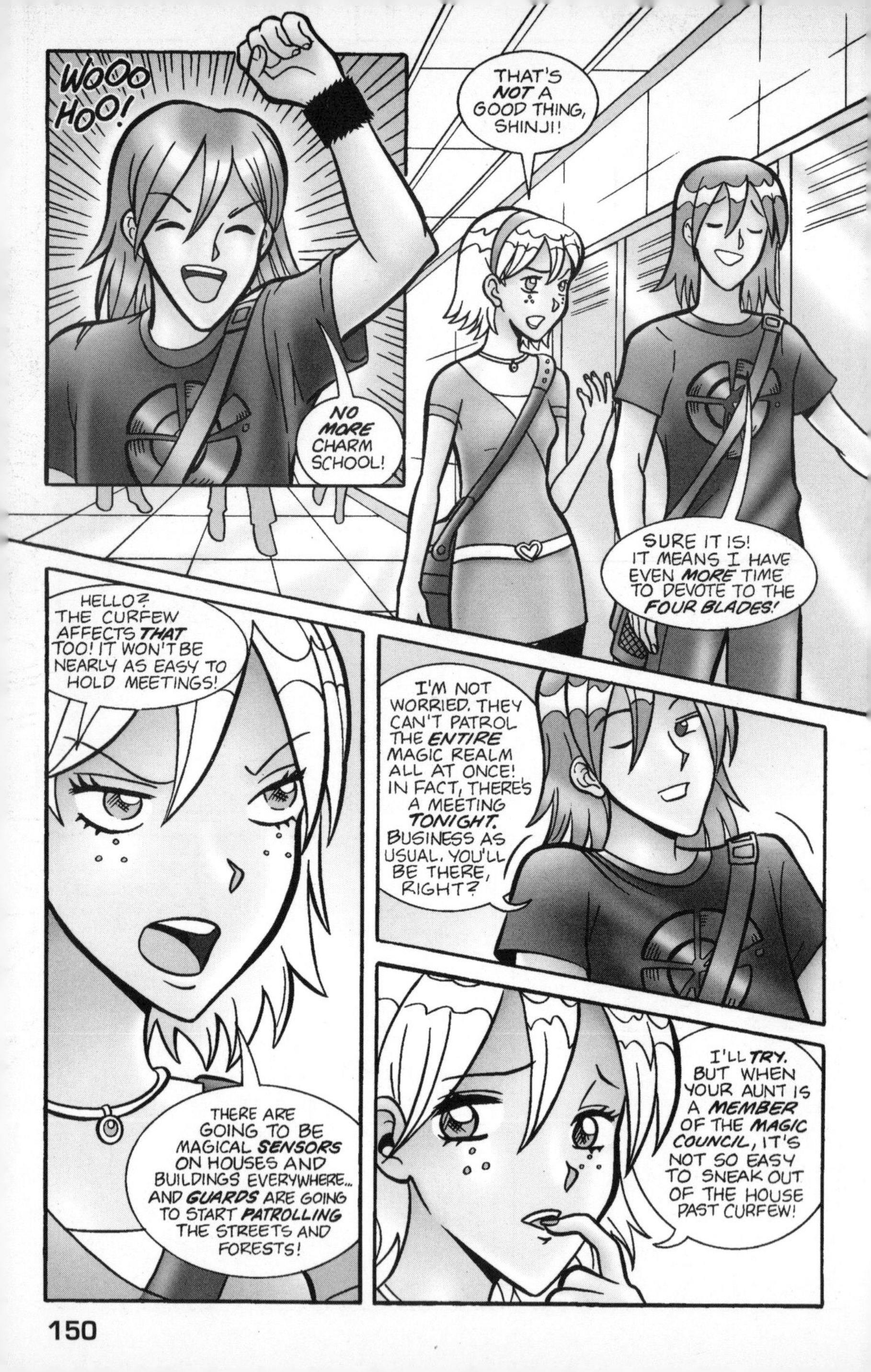
WOOO HOO!
NO MORE CHARM SCHOOL!
THAT'S NOT A GOOD THING, SHINJI!
SURE IT IS! IT MEANS I HAVE EVEN MORE TIME TO DEVOTE TO THE FOUR BLADES!
HELLO? THE CURFEW AFFECTS THAT TOO! IT WON'T BE NEARLY AS EASY TO HOLD MEETINGS!
THERE ARE GOING TO BE MAGICAL SENSORS ON HOUSES AND BUILDINGS EVERYWHERE... AND GUARDS ARE GOING TO START PATROLLING THE STREETS AND FORESTS!
I'M NOT WORRIED. THEY CAN'T PATROL THE ENTIRE MAGIC REALM ALL AT ONCE! IN FACT, THERE'S A MEETING TONIGHT. BUSINESS AS USUAL. YOU'LL BE THERE, RIGHT?
I'LL TRY. BUT WHEN YOUR AUNT IS A MEMBER OF THE MAGIC COUNCIL, IT'S NOT SO EASY TO SNEAK OUT OF THE HOUSE PAST CURFEW!

LEAVE ME, PLEASE.
YOUR HIGHNESS... IN TIMES SUCH AS THESE WE FEEL IT BEST TO KEEP AN EYE ON YOU AT ALL TIMES.
I JUST WISH TO SIT A WHILE IN MY GARDEN IN PEACE... YOU MAY WAIT OUTSIDE THE DOOR... I WILL CALL YOU IF I NEED ANYTHING.

SIGH
IT WILL SOON BE HARDER AND HARDER TO FIND TIME FOR SOLITUDE... WHAT A TROUBLESOME TIME THIS IS!
AT LEAST I CAN STILL ENTER MY TRUE SANCTUARY WHEN I NEED IT MOST...
GOING SOMEWHERE, SELES?

YOU AGAIN!
YOU SHOULD HAVE LISTENED TO YOUR GUARDS, SELES. YOU SHOULD NOT BE ALONE IN THESE DANGEROUS TIMES...
YOU'VE ALREADY TAKEN SO MUCH FROM ME! JUST LEAVE ME BE!
GETTING BRAVE, ARE WE? TALKING BACK, NOW?
IS THIS BECAUSE OF THOSE SO-CALLED FOUR BLADES AGAIN? YOU FORGET WHO YOU'RE DEALING WITH! I DESTROYED THE BLADES ONCE AND I'LL DO IT AGAIN!
ENJOY YOUR LITTLE "SANCTUARY" WHILE YOU HAVE IT. SOON IT, AND EVERYTHING ELSE, WILL BE MINE.

SOUNDS LIKE HILDA, ZELDA AND SALEM ARE WATCHING THE "WITCH'S DOZEN" REALITY SHOW. THEY'LL BE OCCUPIED FOR A WHILE!

I'LL JUST ZAP OUT OF HERE REAL QUICK AND CHECK OUT THE FOUR BLADES MEETING.

WHAT THE--?
FIZZzzzz

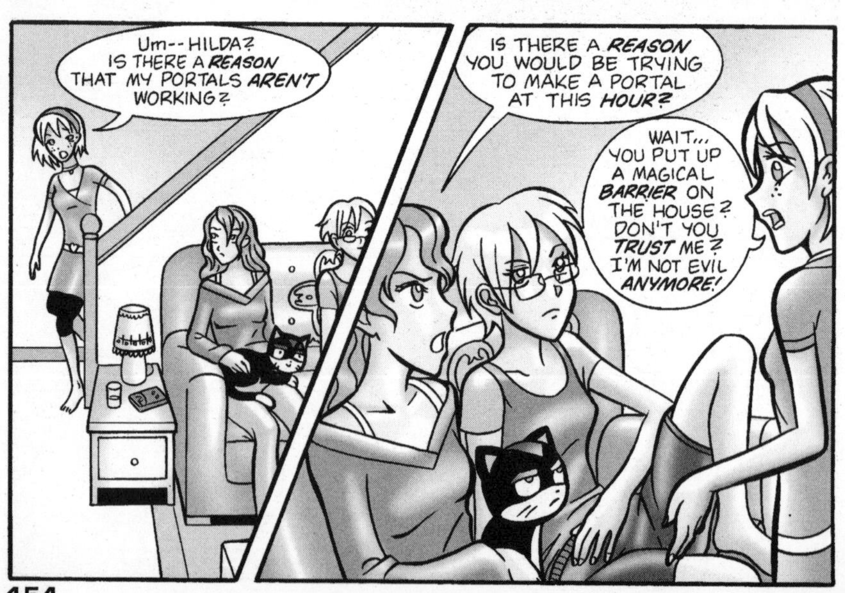
Um--HILDA? IS THERE A REASON THAT MY PORTALS AREN'T WORKING?
IS THERE A REASON YOU WOULD BE TRYING TO MAKE A PORTAL AT THIS HOUR?
WAIT... YOU PUT UP A MAGICAL BARRIER ON THE HOUSE? DON'T YOU TRUST ME? I'M NOT EVIL ANYMORE!

IT'S NOT ABOUT TRUST, SABRINA, IT'S ABOUT THE NEW MAGIC REALM CURFEW.
AS CZARINA OF MEDIATION, IT'S MY JOB TO MAKE SURE THAT NOBODY CAN ENTER THE MAGIC REALM AFTER HOURS. IT'S FOR EVERYONE'S SAFETY.
BUT WHAT ABOUT MY TUTORING SESSIONS WITH BATTY BARTHOLOMEW? HE'S EXPECTING ME!
I'M SORRY, SABRINA. TUTORING IS POSTPONED UNTIL THE CURFEW ENDS. I'M SURE MR. BARTHOLOMEW IS AWARE OF THIS.

BUT--!
SHHH!
THEY'RE ABOUT TO DO THE ELIMINATION ROUND!

WELL, CAN I JUST GO OVER TO LLANDRA'S THEN?
FINE. JUST BE BACK BY YOUR MORTAL CURFEW.

THIS IS GONNA BE HARDER THAN I THOUGHT...
HILDA PUT A BARRIER NOT JUST ON OUR HOUSE BUT IN BETWEEN BOTH REALMS!

SABRINA! I CAN'T GET INTO THE MAGIC REALM! I TOLD NARAYAN I'D PICK HIM UP AND WE'D GO TO THE FOUR BLADES MEETING TOGETHER... HE'S PROBABLY WORRYING ABOUT ME RIGHT NOW!
RELAX... NARAYAN KNOWS ABOUT THE CURFEW. HE'LL KNOW THAT YOU GOT STUCK SOMEWHERE.
YOU'RE RIGHT... I SHOULDN'T FREAK OUT... I JUST HATE NOT BEING ABLE TO CONTACT HIM!
HILDA PUT A BARRIER IN BETWEEN THE REALMS.
THAT MEANS PORTALS DON'T WORK AND FLYING THERE ON BROOMS WON'T WORK EITHER-- WE'LL JUST HIT A WALL.
BUT THERE MUST BE OTHER WAYS INTO THE REALM...
HILDA CAN DETER PEOPLE FROM ENTERING, BUT EVEN SHE DOESN'T HAVE THE POWER TO BLOCK EVERY ENTRANCE AT THE SAME TIME. WE JUST HAVE TO THINK HARDER!
YOUR WAND!
YOU CAN BREAK THROUGH ANYTHING WITH IT! EVEN BARRIERS!
THAT WOULD REQUIRE ME TO USE THE DARK END OF THE WAND... I CAN'T RISK IT. I MIGHT FALL UNDER ITS INFLUENCE AGAIN...

Hmm
I HAVE A CRAZY IDEA!
FOLLOW ME!
MY DAD USED TO BE A SHAMAN IN THE BRAZILIAN RAINFORESTS...
I REMEMBER HE ONCE TOLD ME HOW HE MAGICALLY TRAVELED THROUGH THE ROOT SYSTEM!
WOW, REALLY? ARE YOU SAYING WE CAN GET INTO THE MAGIC REALM THROUGH THE ROOTS?
I DON'T KNOW... I'VE NEVER TRIED IT BEFORE. BUT IT'S WORTH A SHOT!
O ROOTS, TAKE US DEEP UNDERGROUND AND LET US TRAVEL THROUGH YOUR WINDING WAYS UNTIL WE REACH THE LIGHT OF THE MAGIC REALM MOONS.

WAAAAAAHHH!!!
IT'S WORKING, LLANDRA!!
WE'RE NOT THERE YET! JUST HANG ON TIGHT!
ARE WE IN THE MAGIC REALM? DID WE--?
GET DOWN!

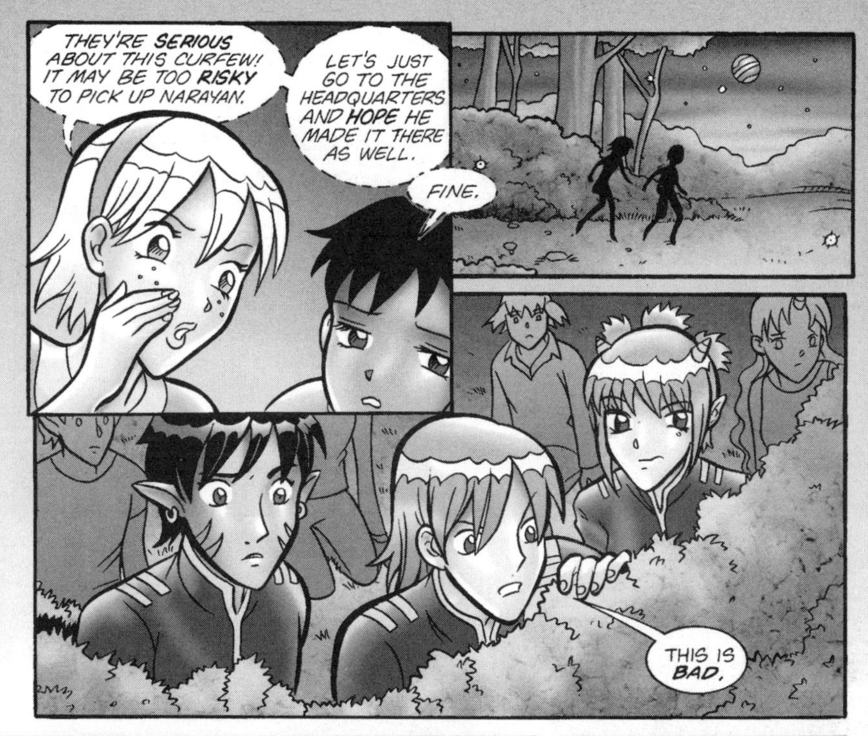
THEY'RE SERIOUS ABOUT THIS CURFEW! IT MAY BE TOO RISKY TO PICK UP NARAYAN.
LET'S JUST GO TO THE HEADQUARTERS AND HOPE HE MADE IT THERE AS WELL.
FINE.
THIS IS BAD.

THANK GOODNESS I PUT A CLOAKING SPELL ON THE STUFF INSIDE... IT WON'T HOLD FOR LONG, THOUGH.

SHINJI! WHAT'S GOING ON?

LLANDRA! YOU'RE *OK!*
SO ARE *YOU!*

BUT... HOW COME YOU DIDN'T *WAIT* FOR ME?
I WAITED AS *LONG* AS I COULD... I THOUGHT YOU WENT *WITHOUT* ME! AND YOU *DID!*

IT DOESN'T *MATTER!*
SEE WHAT HAPPENED, LLANDRA? YOU AND SABRINA HANDED OUT *MEETING CARDS* TO ALL THE MEMBERS OF THE *ORIGINAL* FOUR BLADES AND ONE OF THEM FELL INTO THE *WRONG* HANDS!*
* LAST CHAPTER

IT WAS *WORTH* THE RISK! WE MANAGED TO GET ALMOST *ALL* THE ORIGINAL SURVIVING MEMBERS TO *MEET* WITH US!
AND FOR *WHAT?* THEY ALL RAN OFF WITH YOUR BATTY TUTOR, *BARTHOLOMEW!* HE'S NOT THEIR LEADER--*I AM!*

OBVIOUSLY BATTY HAS SOME SORT OF *SWAY* OVER THOSE MEMBERS.
MAYBE THEY HAVE AN EVEN *BETTER* MEETING PLACE... THE *ORIGINAL* MEETING PLACE THAT THE MAGIC COUNCIL NEVER FOUND! OUR OWN H.Q. WAS NEVER WELL-HIDDEN ENOUGH.
THEY ALWAYS SAY THAT THE *BEST* WAY TO HIDE IS TO DO IT IN *PLAIN* SIGHT... AND IT'S *WORKED* FOR US SO FAR. BUT LLANDRA'S *RIGHT.* WE'VE OUTGROWN THIS PLACE. WE NEED TO FIGURE OUT WHERE BARTHOLOMEW LED THE ORIGINAL MEMBERS.

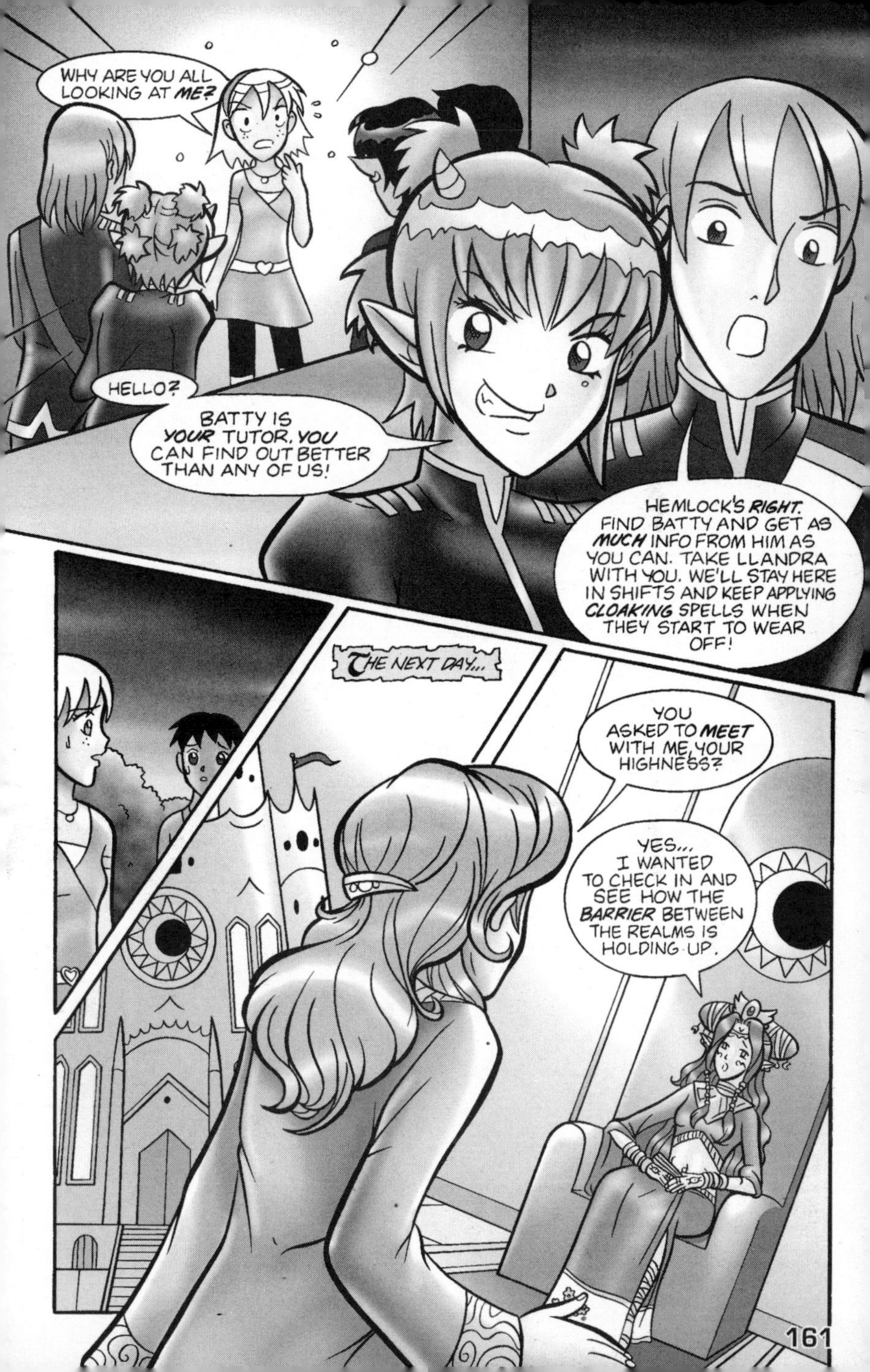
WHY ARE YOU ALL LOOKING AT ME?
HELLO?
BATTY IS YOUR TUTOR. YOU CAN FIND OUT BETTER THAN ANY OF US!
HEMLOCK'S RIGHT. FIND BATTY AND GET AS MUCH INFO FROM HIM AS YOU CAN. TAKE LLANDRA WITH YOU. WE'LL STAY HERE IN SHIFTS AND KEEP APPLYING CLOAKING SPELLS WHEN THEY START TO WEAR OFF!
THE NEXT DAY...
YOU ASKED TO MEET WITH ME, YOUR HIGHNESS?
YES... I WANTED TO CHECK IN AND SEE HOW THE BARRIER BETWEEN THE REALMS IS HOLDING UP.

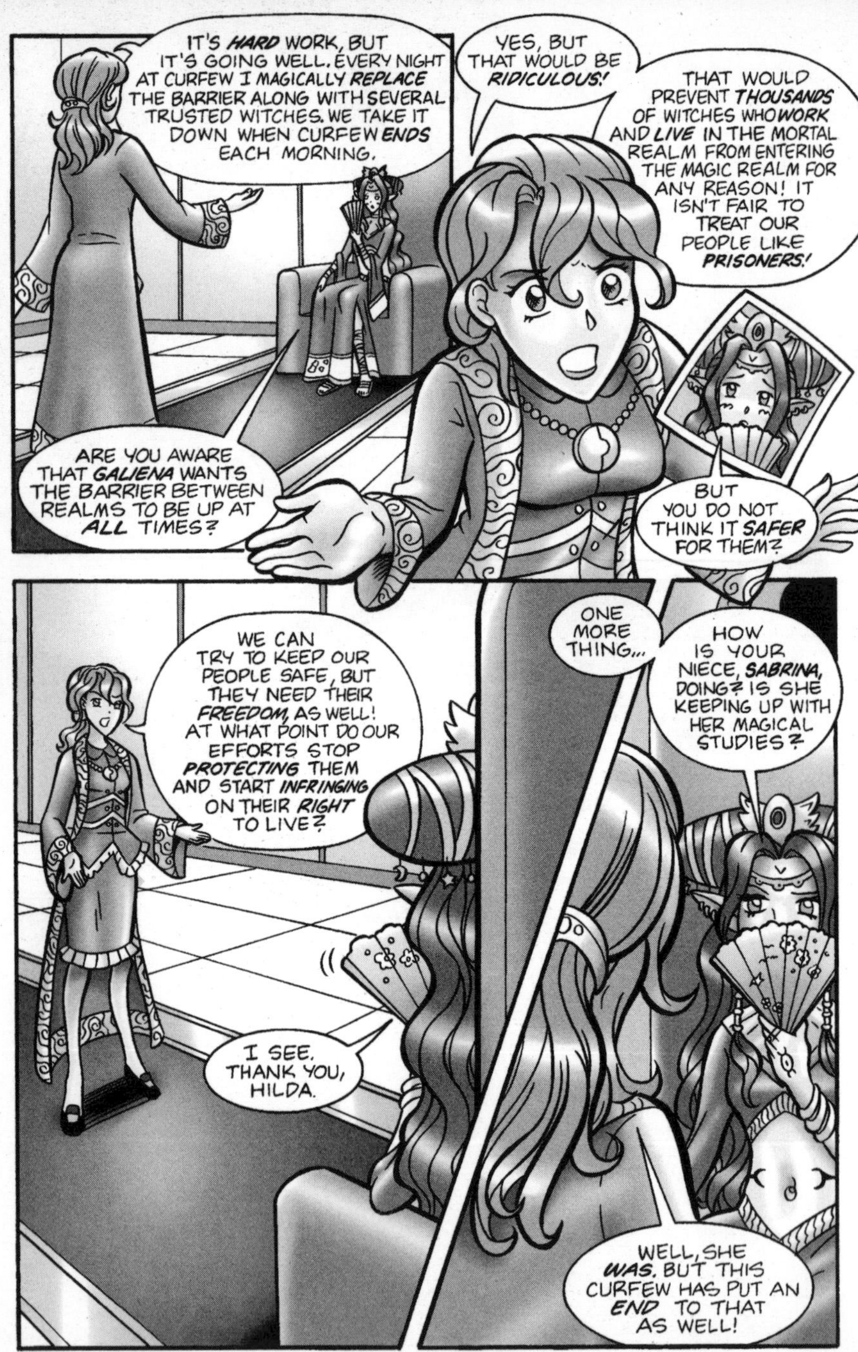
IT'S HARD WORK, BUT IT'S GOING WELL. EVERY NIGHT AT CURFEW I MAGICALLY REPLACE THE BARRIER ALONG WITH SEVERAL TRUSTED WITCHES. WE TAKE IT DOWN WHEN CURFEW ENDS EACH MORNING.
ARE YOU AWARE THAT GALIENA WANTS THE BARRIER BETWEEN REALMS TO BE UP AT ALL TIMES?
YES, BUT THAT WOULD BE RIDICULOUS!
THAT WOULD PREVENT THOUSANDS OF WITCHES WHO WORK AND LIVE IN THE MORTAL REALM FROM ENTERING THE MAGIC REALM FOR ANY REASON! IT ISN'T FAIR TO TREAT OUR PEOPLE LIKE PRISONERS!
BUT YOU DO NOT THINK IT SAFER FOR THEM?
WE CAN TRY TO KEEP OUR PEOPLE SAFE, BUT THEY NEED THEIR FREEDOM, AS WELL! AT WHAT POINT DO OUR EFFORTS STOP PROTECTING THEM AND START INFRINGING ON THEIR RIGHT TO LIVE?
I SEE. THANK YOU, HILDA.
ONE MORE THING...
HOW IS YOUR NIECE, SABRINA, DOING? IS SHE KEEPING UP WITH HER MAGICAL STUDIES?
WELL, SHE WAS. BUT THIS CURFEW HAS PUT AN END TO THAT AS WELL!

HOW UNFORTUNATE.
WILL YOU LET HER KNOW THAT EVEN WHEN SHE CANNOT SEEK TUTELAGE, SHE CAN AT LEAST VISIT THE FOREST OF HER MIND FOR ANSWERS?
Uh... SURE.
ONLY A COUPLE OF HOURS LEFT 'TIL CURFEW... I HOPE BATTY'S HOME!
I JUST HOPE HE'S WILLING TO TALK TO US!
I WONDER IF THE ORIGINAL BLADES MEET AT HIS HOUSE? IT'S HARD ENOUGH TO GET TO!
THAT'S FOR SURE! EVEN THE GUARDS DON'T PATROL OUT THIS FAR!
WHICH MEANS WE HAVE TO BE EXTRA CAREFUL ABOUT THE MONSTERS...

KNOCK
KNOCK
YOU KNOW, MY HOUSE HAS BEEN VERY MESSY SINCE YOU STOPPED COMING HERE, SERENA!
FWOOSH
IT'S SABRINA. AND I'M NOT YOUR MAID, I'M YOUR STUDENT! I RESTORED YOUR MEMORY! YOU SHOULD KNOW THIS!
OH, YES. THAT'S RIGHT. WELL, I'M STILL GOING TO HAVE TO GIVE YOU AN "F" FOR THIS WEEK.
WHAT?! WHY?
NON-ATTENDANCE!

BUT WITH THE CURFEW, IT'S BEEN IMPOSSIBLE TO COME HERE, BATTY! YOU KNOW THAT!
YEAH? WELL, YOU'RE NOT MY MOM! I CAN STAY OUT AS LONG AS I LIKE!

LOOK, BATTY, THE REASON WE'RE HERE IS BECAUSE WE NEED ANSWERS! ABOUT THE FOUR BLADES!
WHY DID YOU AND THE ORIGINAL BLADES STORM OUT OF THE LAST MEETING? WHY WON'T YOU JOIN OUR CAUSE?
WE'RE TWO GENERATIONS FIGHTING FOR THE SAME CAUSE! WE CAN WORK TOGETHER!

WHY? WHY WON'T YOU EXPLAIN THIS TO US?
WRONG!
WHAM!

I TOLD YOU... THE ORIGINAL BLADES AND I... WE ARE SWORN TO SECRECY!
IF YOU WANT ANSWERS, YOU MUST SEEK THEM YOURSELF...
IN THE FOREST OF YOUR MIND!
LET'S GO, LLANDRA!
HE'S AS BATTY AS EVER!
SHINJI'S NOT GOING TO BE HAPPY ABOUT THIS!
WHAT DOES HE EXPECT US TO DO? IT'S IMPOSSIBLE TO REASON WITH BATTY!
WELL... WE TRIED. LET'S GET BACK BEFORE THE CURFEW ENDS.
WAIT, LLANDRA! I WANT TO SHOW YOU SOMETHING AMAZING!
I FOUND THIS THE LAST TIME I WAS HERE, BUT IT WAS TOO RISKY TO FULLY EXPLORE ON MY OWN.
ZAP

WHAT IS THIS PLACE?
YOU'LL SEE!

WOW!!
I KNOW, RIGHT?!

LET'S SEE WHAT'S ON BOARD!
ARE YOU SURE IT'S SAFE?
I HAVE MY WAND IF WE RUN INTO TROUBLE!

CAREFUL, THERE'S HOLES EVERYWHERE.
LOOK AT THOSE CRATES! THINK THERE'S TREASURE IN THEM?

ONLY ONE WAY TO FIND OUT!

OLD... RUGS?

UGH...
MOLDY TEA AND SPICES.

WELL, THIS MASK IS PRETTY COOL, AT LEAST!

WAAAAAH!

AAAAAAAAAHHH!!!

DID THAT JUST HAPPEN?!
Uh, uh... YEAH!
THINK THEY ALL DO THAT?!
YOU CAN TRY ONE AND FIND OUT!
NO WAY!

THE RUGS!
THEY'RE FLOATING!
FLYING CARPETS!!
WEEEE!
WE FOUND TREASURE AFTER ALL!
OR HAVE WE? THESE ITEMS COULD BE CURSED... JUST LIKE YOUR WAND. WE HAVE TO BE CAREFUL...
YEAH... YOU'RE RIGHT.
WE DON'T EVEN KNOW WHOSE SHIP THIS WAS...
YET ANOTHER MYSTERY THAT NEEDS ANSWERS...
To be continued...

WILL SABRINA EVER GET A STRAIGHT ANSWER OUT OF **BATTY BARTHOLOMEW**?

CAN **THE FOUR BLADES** HOPE TO UNRAVEL THE SECRETS BEFORE THEM AND SAVE **THE MAGIC REALM**?

Chapter 8

Remembrance part 3
SO, AS HISTORY SHOWS IN THIS CASE, THE LARGEST, MOST DESTRUCTIVE WARS CAN BE SPURRED BY MISINFORMATION. THERE IS ALMOST ALWAYS MORE TO THE SITUATION THAN MEETS THE EYE. IF WE HAD THE OPPORTUNITY TO RE-WRITE HISTORY, WHO CAN TELL ME WHAT THE GOVERNMENT COULD HAVE DONE BETTER TO AVOID THIS OUTCOME?
WRITER · TANIA DEL RIO
PENCILS · LINDSAY CIBOS
INKS · JIM AMASH
COLORS · JASON JENSEN
LETTERS · TERESA DAVIDSON
EDITOR/MANAGING EDITOR MIKE PELLERITO
EDITOR-IN-CHIEF VICTOR GORELICK

THEY COULD HAVE BEEN MORE HONEST WITH THE PEOPLE?

GOOD, THAT'S ONE THING. SOMETIMES A GOVERNMENT, IN ITS EFFORT TO PROTECT THE PEOPLE, CAN CONCEAL TOO MUCH FROM THEM, LEADING TO DISTRUST. WHAT ELSE?

SHINJI, I'VE NEVER SEEN YOU THIS DEPRESSED. WHAT'S WRONG?!

THE FOUR BLADES. I GIVE UP.
WAIT A MINUTE! HOW COME?

I GIVE UP.
WHAT?

MY GOAL WAS TO BE READY BY FOUR BLADES DAY.
BUT IT'S ALMOST HERE AND I FEEL LIKE THERE'S NO WAY WE CAN WIN. I WANTED IT TO BE A COMPLETE SURPRISE--SOMETHING THE MAGIC COUNCIL WOULD NEVER EXPECT!
BUT THE MAGIC COUNCIL IS ONTO US!
WE'VE ALREADY BEEN FORCED TO ABANDON OUR FIRST HIDEOUT, AND WITH THE NEW CURFEW, IT'S IMPOSSIBLE TO FIND A NEW PLACE FOR EVERYONE TO MEET IN SECRET.
NOT ONLY THAT, BUT BATTY HAS ALL THE ORIGINAL FOUR BLADES MEMBERS AND THEY WON'T COOPERATE* WE DON'T EVEN HAVE THE FALLEN MANA LEAF ANYMORE! THERE'S JUST TOO MUCH STANDING IN MY WAY!
*LAST CHAPTER

I GIVE UP.

MAYBE HE'S RIGHT. MAYBE THIS IS FOR THE BEST.
IT'S SO **DANGEROUS** WHAT WE'VE BEEN PLANNING TO DO... IF WE FAIL WE COULD END UP **DEAD** OR WITH OUR MEMORIES **WIPED.**

BUT THIS IS SO **IMPORTANT** TO SHINJI...
HE **LOST** HIS PARENTS BECAUSE OF THE FOUR BLADES AND HE NEEDS TO **FINISH** WHAT THEY STARTED...
I KNOW **I** WOULD. MY DAD WAS A **MEMBER** TOO...

DON'T GIVE UP, SHINJI.
WE'VE COME **TOO FAR** TO STOP NOW! WHO **CARES** IF THE MAGIC COUNCIL SUSPECTS SOMETHING? WE CAN **STILL** BEAT THEM!
BUT **HOW?**

I THINK I FOUND SOMETHING THAT MIGHT HELP, TOMORROW NIGHT, AFTER CURFEW, MEET ME AND LLANDRA AT HER PLACE.
HEY, 'BRINA! GOOD DAY?
IT WAS OKAY. IN ENGLISH WE STARTED TO--

COOL! WELL, I'M OFF TO THE PET STORE TO PICK UP SOME CAT FOOD. ZAP UP SOME DINNER BEFORE HILDA GETS HOME, WILL YOU?
Uhh... OK...

THERE'S SOMETHING FISHY ABOUT ZELDA LATELY.

WHAT DO YOU MEAN?
SHE GOES TO THE PET STORE ALMOST EVERY DAY BUT SHE DOESN'T LET ME GO WITH HER! HALF THE TIME SHE DOESN'T COME BACK WITH CAT FOOD!
Huh... THAT IS WEIRD...

ARE YOU SURE THIS IS A GOOD IDEA? DO WE REALLY WANT TO KNOW WHAT SHE'S UP TO?
HEY, I JUST WANT MY CAT FOOD! WHAT ZELDA DOES IS HER BUSINESS, BUT WHEN SHE FORGETS MY DINNER, IT'S PERSONAL!
WELL, SO FAR, SHE'S HEADING TOWARDS THE PET STORE.
ON Sale!
DELI HAM
Hmm... WELL, THERE'S STILL TIME. KEEP FOLLOWING HER!
DON'T LOSE SIGHT OF HER! SHE MIGHT TRY TO TELEPORT!
Pets R Us
OR... SHE MIGHT JUST TRY TO GO TO THE PET STORE!

SEE, SALEM? YOU'RE JUST BEING PARANOID! NOW I'D BETTER GET HOME AND ZAP DINNER BEFORE ZELDA GETS BACK!
WAIT, LET'S PEEK IN THE WINDOW.
SIGH...
THIS IS RIDICULOUS. YOU KNOW THAT, RIGHT?
WHOA...

Rex
MEOW

SHE'S GONE TO THE DARK SIDE!
FIRST YOU, AND NOW ZELDA!

DON'T BE SILLY! ATTICUS REX ISN'T EVIL ANYMORE!
HE HAD HIS MEMORY WIPED, REMEMBER?* HE'S JUST A REGULAR GUY NOW!
* SEE BOOK 1

Rex

=SIGH= ... I THINK IT'S CUTE!
I THINK IT'S TROUBLE!

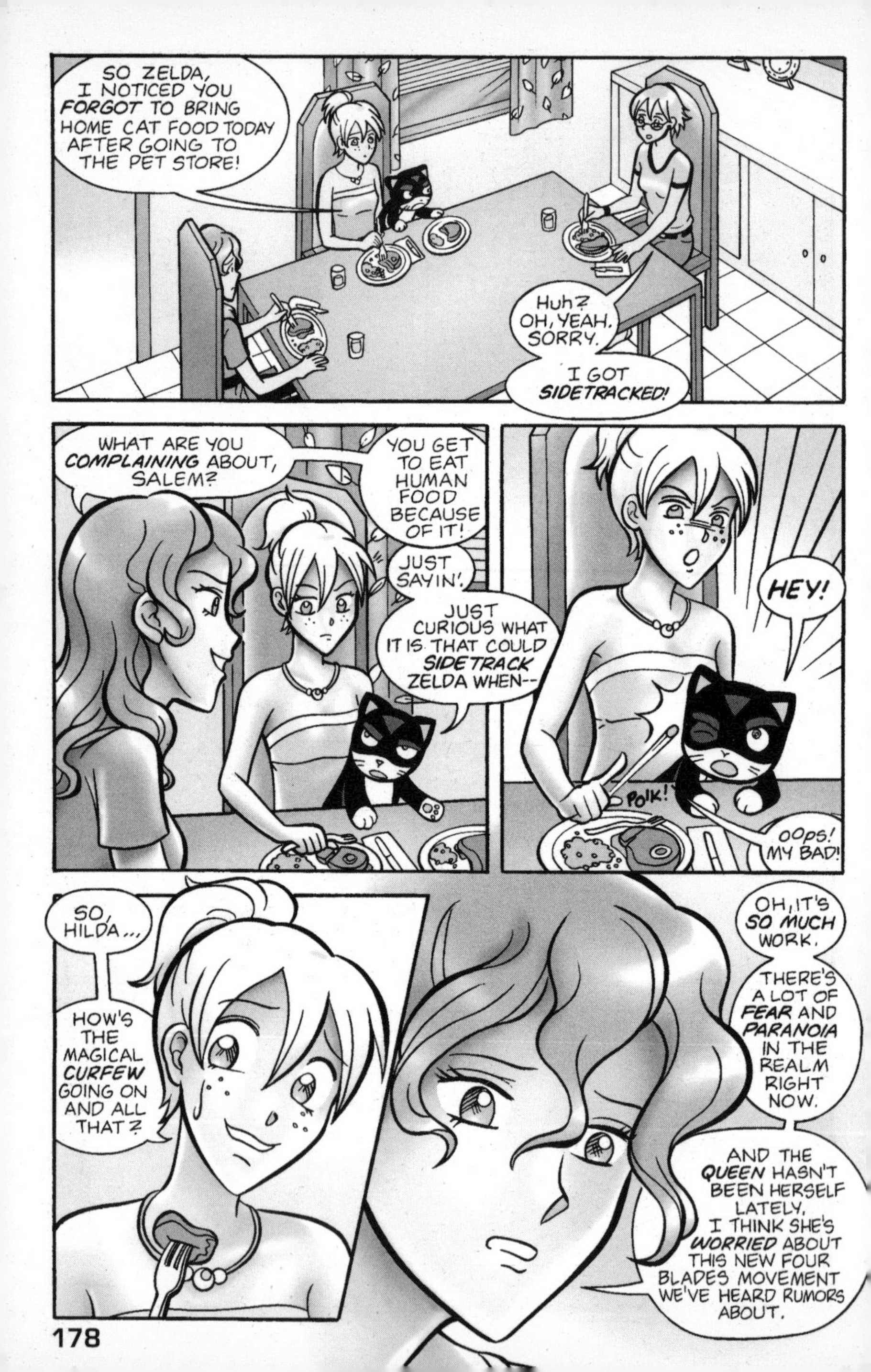
SO ZELDA, I NOTICED YOU FORGOT TO BRING HOME CAT FOOD TODAY AFTER GOING TO THE PET STORE!
Huh? OH, YEAH. SORRY.
I GOT SIDETRACKED!
WHAT ARE YOU COMPLAINING ABOUT, SALEM?
YOU GET TO EAT HUMAN FOOD BECAUSE OF IT!
JUST SAYIN'.
JUST CURIOUS WHAT IT IS THAT COULD SIDETRACK ZELDA WHEN--
HEY!
POIK!
OOPS! MY BAD!
SO, HILDA...
HOW'S THE MAGICAL CURFEW GOING ON AND ALL THAT?
OH, IT'S SO MUCH WORK.
THERE'S A LOT OF FEAR AND PARANOIA IN THE REALM RIGHT NOW.
AND THE QUEEN HASN'T BEEN HERSELF LATELY. I THINK SHE'S WORRIED ABOUT THIS NEW FOUR BLADES MOVEMENT WE'VE HEARD RUMORS ABOUT.

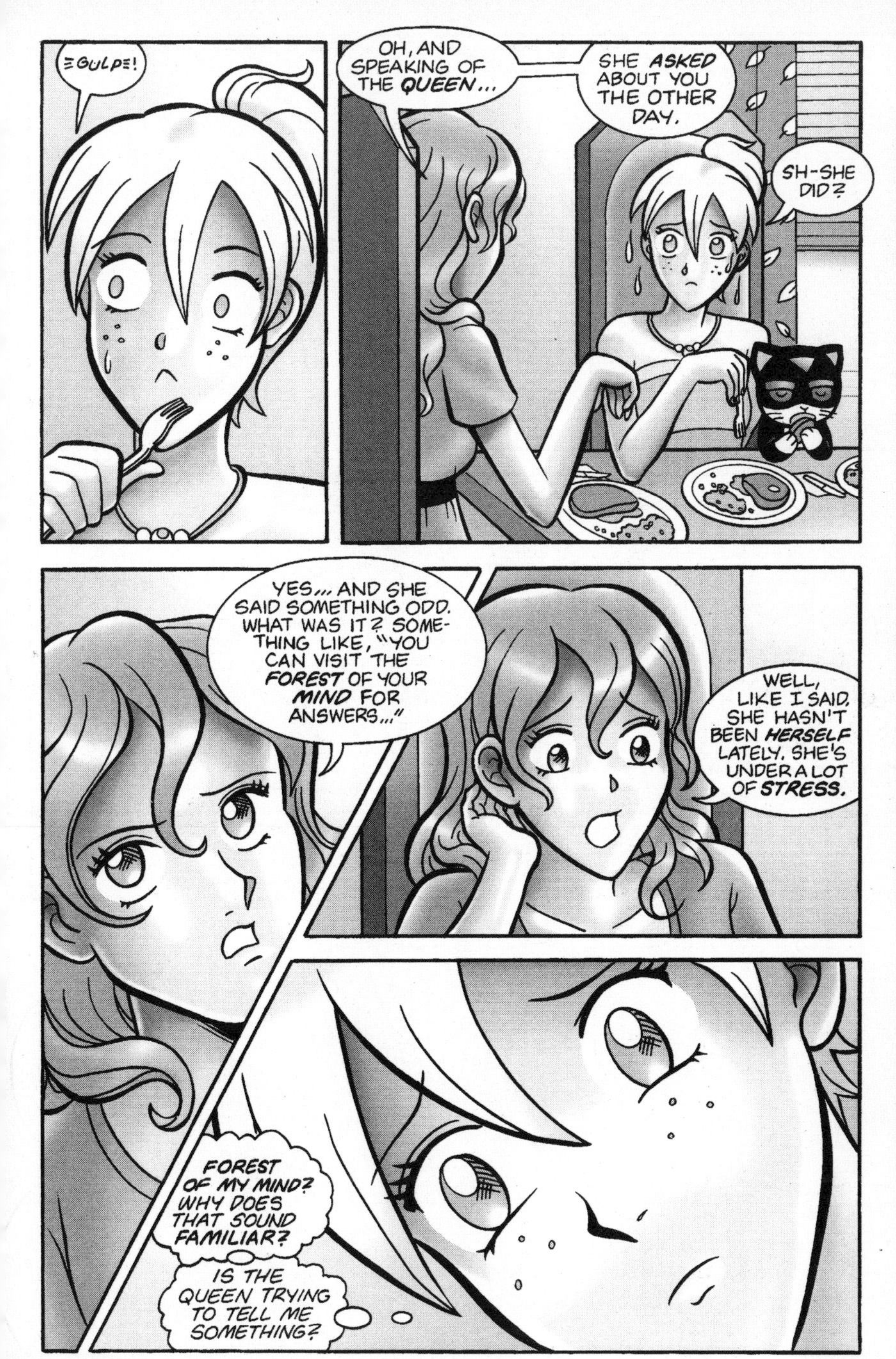

≡GULP≡!
OH, AND SPEAKING OF THE QUEEN...
SHE ASKED ABOUT YOU THE OTHER DAY.
SH-SHE DID?
YES... AND SHE SAID SOMETHING ODD. WHAT WAS IT? SOMETHING LIKE, "YOU CAN VISIT THE FOREST OF YOUR MIND FOR ANSWERS..."
WELL, LIKE I SAID, SHE HASN'T BEEN HERSELF LATELY. SHE'S UNDER A LOT OF STRESS.
FOREST OF MY MIND? WHY DOES THAT SOUND FAMILIAR?
IS THE QUEEN TRYING TO TELL ME SOMETHING?

HEY, LLANDRA, TOMORROW NIGHT I THINK WE'RE GONNA SHOW SHINJI THAT PLACE! I THINK IT WILL HELP, DON'T YOU?
YEAH! THINK WE CAN TRY THE ROOT SYSTEM AGAIN? *
* LAST CHAPTER
Uhhhh! GOTTA GO! BYE!

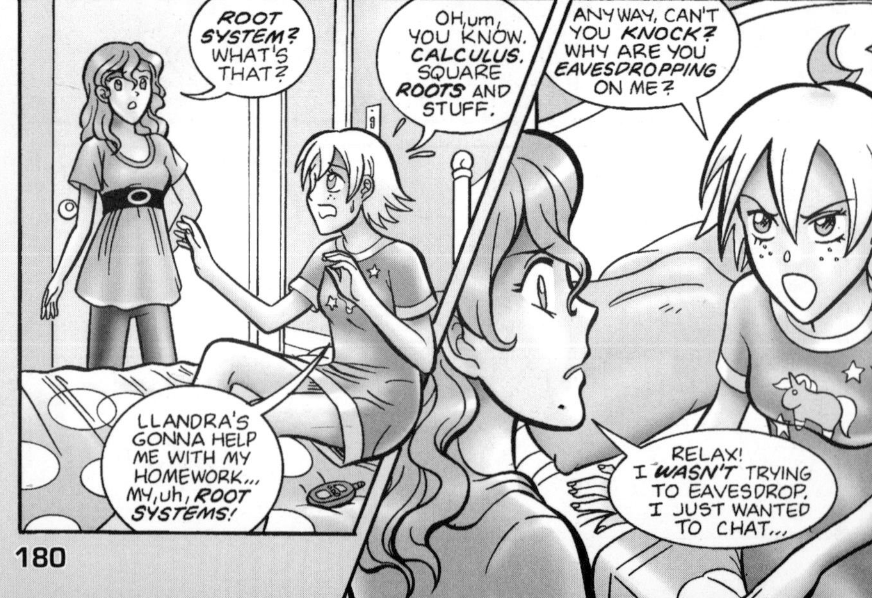
ROOT SYSTEM? WHAT'S THAT?
LLANDRA'S GONNA HELP ME WITH MY HOMEWORK... MY, uh, ROOT SYSTEMS!
OH, um, YOU KNOW. CALCULUS. SQUARE ROOTS AND STUFF.
ANYWAY, CAN'T YOU KNOCK? WHY ARE YOU EAVESDROPPING ON ME?
RELAX! I WASN'T TRYING TO EAVESDROP. I JUST WANTED TO CHAT...

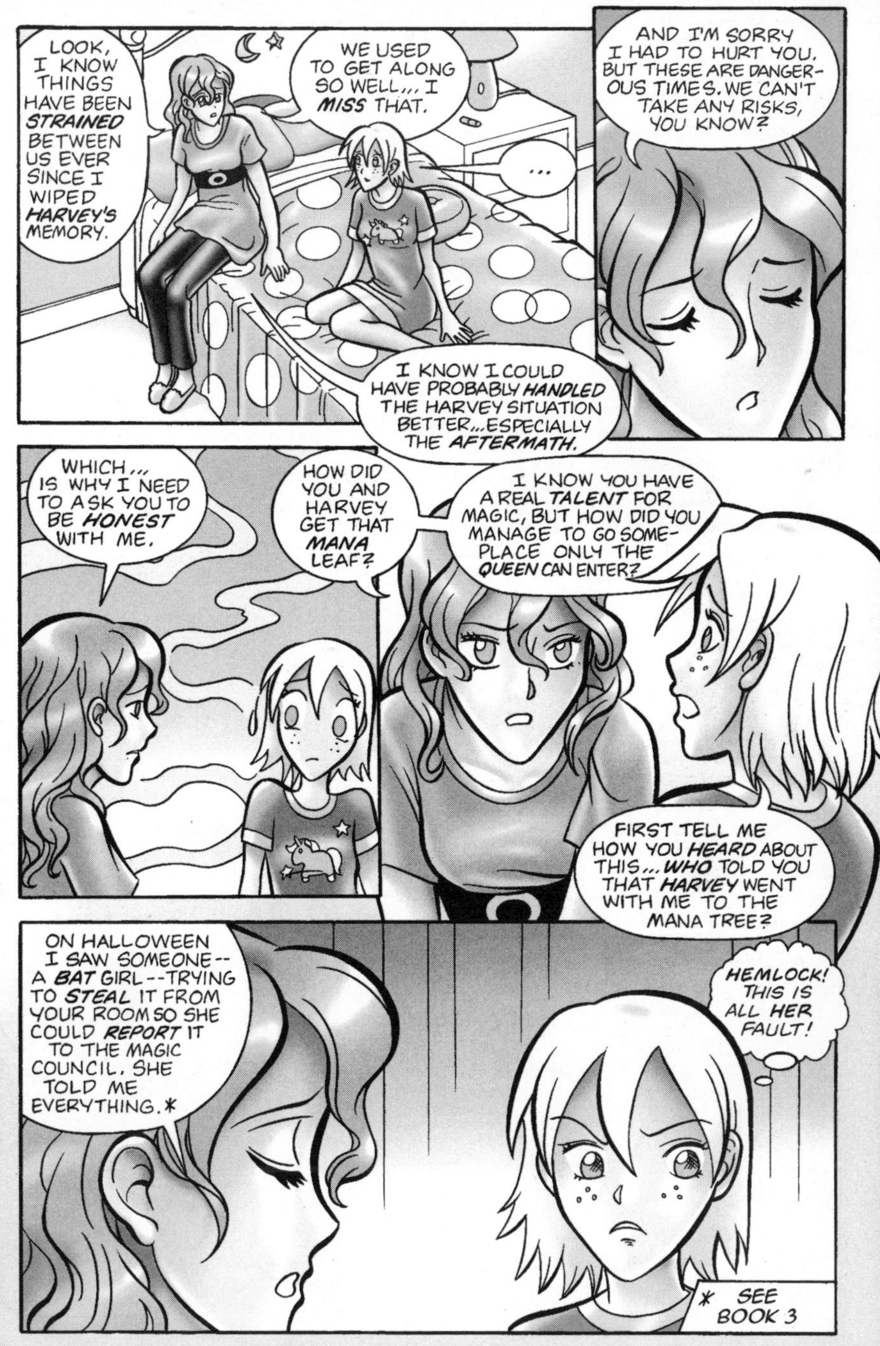
LOOK, I KNOW THINGS HAVE BEEN STRAINED BETWEEN US EVER SINCE I WIPED HARVEY'S MEMORY.
WE USED TO GET ALONG SO WELL... I MISS THAT.
...
I KNOW I COULD HAVE PROBABLY HANDLED THE HARVEY SITUATION BETTER... ESPECIALLY THE AFTERMATH.
AND I'M SORRY I HAD TO HURT YOU. BUT THESE ARE DANGEROUS TIMES. WE CAN'T TAKE ANY RISKS, YOU KNOW?
WHICH... IS WHY I NEED TO ASK YOU TO BE HONEST WITH ME.
HOW DID YOU AND HARVEY GET THAT MANA LEAF?
I KNOW YOU HAVE A REAL TALENT FOR MAGIC, BUT HOW DID YOU MANAGE TO GO SOMEPLACE ONLY THE QUEEN CAN ENTER?
FIRST TELL ME HOW YOU HEARD ABOUT THIS... WHO TOLD YOU THAT HARVEY WENT WITH ME TO THE MANA TREE?
ON HALLOWEEN I SAW SOMEONE-- A BAT GIRL--TRYING TO STEAL IT FROM YOUR ROOM SO SHE COULD REPORT IT TO THE MAGIC COUNCIL. SHE TOLD ME EVERYTHING.*
HEMLOCK! THIS IS ALL HER FAULT!
* SEE BOOK 3

HOW MUCH SHOULD I TELL HILDA? I CAN'T FORGET THAT SHE'S A MEMBER OF THE MAGIC COUNCIL. SHE'S PUT HER JOB BEFORE ME BEFORE, AND SHE'LL DO IT AGAIN. I HAVE TO BE CAREFUL.

I DON'T KNOW HOW HARVEY AND I WERE ALLOWED TO SEE THE MANA TREE... WE JUST WERE. BUT DID HEMLOCK TAKE THE LEAF? DID SHE BRING IT TO THE MAGIC COUNCIL?
HEMLOCK? YOU MEAN THE BAT GIRL? YOU KNOW HER? NO, I CHASED HER OUT AND KEPT THE LEAF.

YOU STILL HAVE IT? WHERE IS IT? DOES ANYONE KNOW?
NO, IT'S IN A SAFE PLACE. LOOK, SABRINA... THE REAL QUESTION I WANT TO ASK IS THIS...

THE MANA TREE IS IMMORTAL. IT DOESN'T EVEN SHED LEAVES. SO WHY DID YOU TAKE ONE? AND MORE IMPORTANTLY, HOW DID YOU MANAGE TO KILL IT? WHY WOULD YOU DO SUCH A THING?
KILL IT? ME? I DIDN'T KILL IT! IT WAS ALREADY THAT WAY!

DON'T LIE TO ME, SABRINA! THAT'S RIDICULOUS!
WHAT? SO YOU'D RATHER BELIEVE THAT I COULD HAVE THE POWER TO KILL A MANA LEAF? WHAT DO YOU THINK I AM, A MONSTER?
I SAW WHAT THAT WAND DID TO YOU! I WOULDN'T PUT IT PAST YOU!

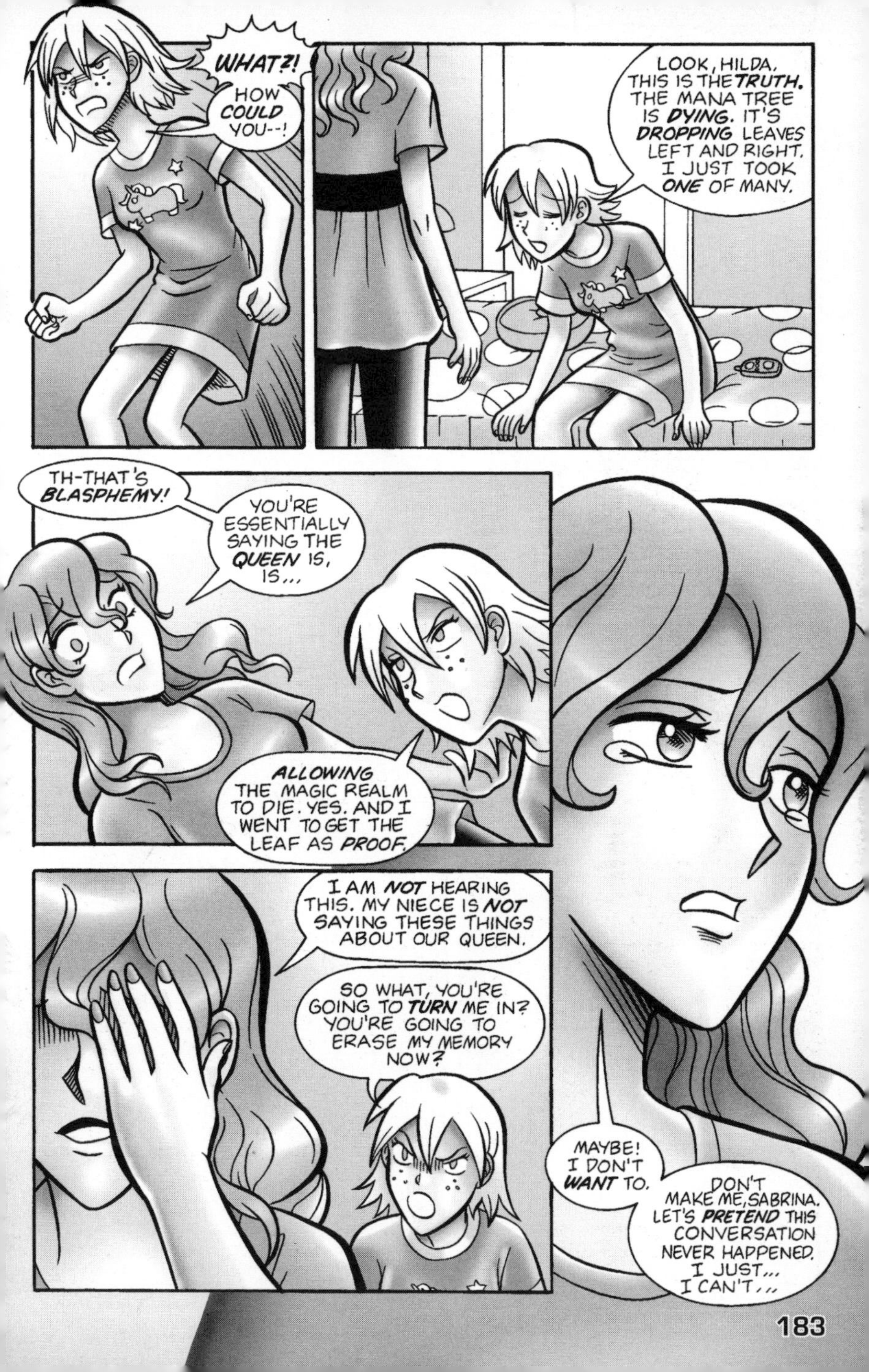
WHAT?!
HOW COULD YOU--!
LOOK, HILDA, THIS IS THE TRUTH. THE MANA TREE IS DYING. IT'S DROPPING LEAVES LEFT AND RIGHT. I JUST TOOK ONE OF MANY.
TH-THAT'S BLASPHEMY!
YOU'RE ESSENTIALLY SAYING THE QUEEN IS, IS...
ALLOWING THE MAGIC REALM TO DIE. YES. AND I WENT TO GET THE LEAF AS PROOF.
I AM NOT HEARING THIS. MY NIECE IS NOT SAYING THESE THINGS ABOUT OUR QUEEN.
SO WHAT, YOU'RE GOING TO TURN ME IN? YOU'RE GOING TO ERASE MY MEMORY NOW?
MAYBE! I DON'T WANT TO.
DON'T MAKE ME, SABRINA. LET'S PRETEND THIS CONVERSATION NEVER HAPPENED. I JUST... I CAN'T...

IT'S A LOT FOR HER TO TAKE IN, BUT I HOPE SHE BELIEVES ME... OR ELSE I'M IN BIG TROUBLE.
IT WON'T BE LONG BEFORE HILDA LINKS ME TO THE FOUR BLADES AND THEN SHE'LL REALLY GO BERSERK.
ARE YOU SURE TRAVELING TO THE MAGIC REALM THROUGH THE ROOT SYSTEM IS SAFE? I WON'T GET STUCK HALFWAY, WILL I?
LOOK, IT'S THE ONLY WAY TO GET INTO THE MAGIC REALM AFTER CURFEW! ALL OTHER ENTRANCES ARE MAGICALLY BLOCKED!

BUT I LIVE IN THE MAGIC REALM! I COULD HAVE JUST MET YOU GUYS ON THE OTHER SIDE!
NOT WHERE WE'RE GOING. NOW, GET READY!

WAAAAH! THIS FEELS... SO... WRONG!
ALMOST THERE!

≡GASP≡...
I AM NEVER DOING THAT AGAIN!
NEITHER AM I! GET ME OUT OF HERE!
Ugh! WHAT A WAY TO TRAVEL! I FEEL ALL STRETCHED OUT!
THERE! THAT'S BETTER!
ZAP!
SHINJI! YOU BROUGHT HEMLOCK!
WHAT? SHE'S MY GIRLFRIEND!
SHE'S A TRAITOR!
YOU TRIED TO STEAL THE MANA LEAF FROM MY ROOM! YOU'RE WORKING AGAINST US!
PROVE IT!
I DON'T HAVE TO! I KNOW YOUR LITTLE GAME!

ENOUGH, YOU TWO! LOOK, I DON'T KNOW IF I WANT TO CONTINUE WITH THE FOUR BLADES.
BUT IF I DO, HEMLOCK IS PART OF IT, WHETHER YOU LIKE IT OR NOT!
DON'T YOU SEE? SHE WANTS THE FOUR BLADES TO FAIL! IF YOU GIVE UP, SHE'LL GET EXACTLY WHAT SHE WANTS!
STOP BICKERING, GUYS!
IT'S DANGEROUS TO BE HERE-- NONE OF US CAN USE MAGIC, EXCEPT FOR SABRINA AND HER WAND. WITH ALL THE MONSTERS LURKING AROUND, I DON'T WANT TO WASTE MY TIME! LET'S GO!
WHAT CAN I SAY, SABRINA? LOVE IS BLIND!
WHAT... WHAT IS THIS?!
LOOK! SEE THESE RUGS? THEY ALL FLY!
AND THESE MASKS? THEY TURN THE WEARER INTO ANIMALS! THERE'S ALSO MAGIC SCROLLS WITH UNDISCOVERED SPELLS! ALL THESE THINGS CAN HELP THE FOUR BLADES!

WOW! THIS IS AMAZING! ALL THESE THINGS WILL HELP US BUILD AN ARMY! A FLYING, MASKED ARMY WITH NEW SPELLS AT OUR DISPOSAL! THE QUEEN WILL NEVER KNOW WHAT HIT HER!
SEE? I TOLD YOU! YOU CAN'T GIVE UP NOW!
THANK YOU, SABRINA. THANK YOU SO MUCH.
WAIT! THIS STUFF COULD BE CURSED! WE DON'T WANT TO TAKE ANY RISKS.
I THOUGHT YOU LIKED TAKING RISKS!

THERE'S JUST SOMETHING ABOUT THIS PLACE... I CAN'T EXPLAIN IT...
M-MOTHER!
WHAT?

MY MOTHER'S SHIP!
HER NAME WAS NOCTURNA... SHE WAS A PIRATE! THAT'S HER EMBLEM! AND THIS IS HER TREASURE!
YOU CAN'T HAVE IT! THIS ISN'T YOURS! GET OUT OF HERE!
HEMLOCK, WAIT! WOULDN'T YOUR MOTHER WANT US TO USE THIS STUFF FOR OUR CAUSE?
NO! I WON'T LET YOU USE MY MOTHER LIKE THIS! GET OFF HER SHIP!
OK, HOLD ON.
I KNOW THIS IS EMOTIONAL FOR YOU. LET'S JUST TAKE A TIME OUT...
DON'T TOUCH ME!
VOSBLANC! I NEED YOU! GET THEM OUT OF HERE!

WHO WAS SHE TALKING TO?
WHAT'S GOTTEN INTO HER?
WE'RE SURROUNDED! WHERE DID THEY ALL COME FROM?
GRRR
GRRR
HEMLOCK! SHE SUMMONED THEM, OR SOMETHING!
GRR
USE YOUR WAND, SABRINA! BLAST THEM!
BUT I'LL HAVE TO USE THE DARK END! WHAT IF I TURN EVIL AGAIN?
JUST DO IT, SABRINA! WE NEED YOU!
FINE! I'LL HOLD THEM OFF, BUT YOU GUYS TAKE A MAGIC CARPET AND JET!
WE'RE NOT LEAVING WITHOUT YOU!
BLAST!

JUST DO IT! GO!
ZAP
BLAST
ZAP
SABRINA! DON'T FIGHT THEM ALL! GET AWAY WHILE YOU CAN!
HANG IN THERE! WE BELIEVE IN YOU!
I'M WAY OUTNUMBERED! AND THE MORE I USE THIS WAND TO DESTROY THEM, THE MORE EVIL I BECOME!
I NEED TO GET AWAY. I NEED TO BE SOMEWHERE SAFE... A SANCTUARY...

Huh?

YOU FOUND YOUR WAY BACK. TO THE FOREST OF OUR MINDS. OUR SANCTUARY.
B-BUT HOW? I DIDN'T EVEN USE MAGIC!

YOU DON'T NEED MAGIC TO COME TO THIS PLACE.
REMEMBER THE LAST TIME YOU WERE HERE? YOU MANAGED TO ESCAPE YOUR PRISON CELL WHICH HAD A MAGIC BLOCK OVER IT.* THIS PLACE IS SPECIAL. IT EXISTS OUTSIDE OF MAGIC. IT EXISTS IN OUR HEARTS. AND IT WILL BE HERE AS LONG AS YOU NEED A PLACE TO GET AWAY... AND TO GET ANSWERS.
* SEE BOOK 3

ANSWERS? THEN I HAVE A QUESTION FOR YOU, QUEEN SELES!
WHY ARE YOU ALLOWING THE MAGIC REALM TO DIE? WHY IS THE MANA TREE WITHERING?

NO ONE HAS EVER BEEN BRAVE ENOUGH TO ASK ME THAT QUESTION, SABRINA. THOSE WHO KNOW LOOK THE OTHER WAY, AND THOSE WHO SUSPECT WOULD NEVER DARE TO SAY SUCH A THING TO ME. IT WOULD BE TREASON.

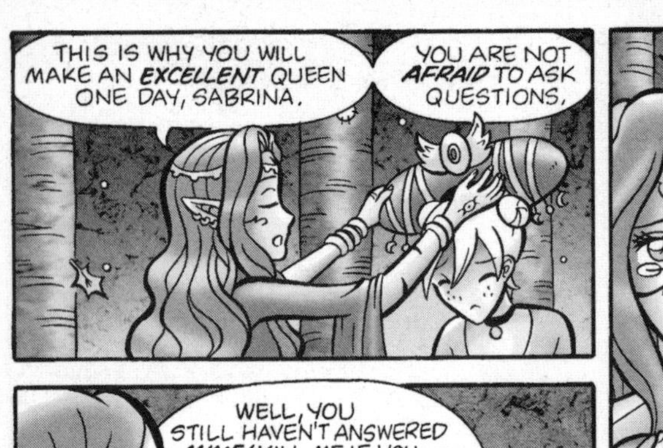
THIS IS WHY YOU WILL MAKE AN EXCELLENT QUEEN ONE DAY, SABRINA.
YOU ARE NOT AFRAID TO ASK QUESTIONS.

KILL YOU? EVEN IF I WANTED TO, I WOULDN'T BE ABLE TO LIFT A FINGER AGAINST YOU. YOUR MAGIC FAR SURPASSES MY OWN!
TH-THAT'S IMPOSSIBLE! THE QUEEN IS THE MOST SKILLED MAGIC USER IN THE REALM. THAT'S THE MAIN REASON YOU ARE THE QUEEN!

WELL, YOU STILL HAVEN'T ANSWERED MINE! KILL ME IF YOU WANT, BUT TELL ME WHY YOU'RE LETTING THE MAGIC REALM DIE!

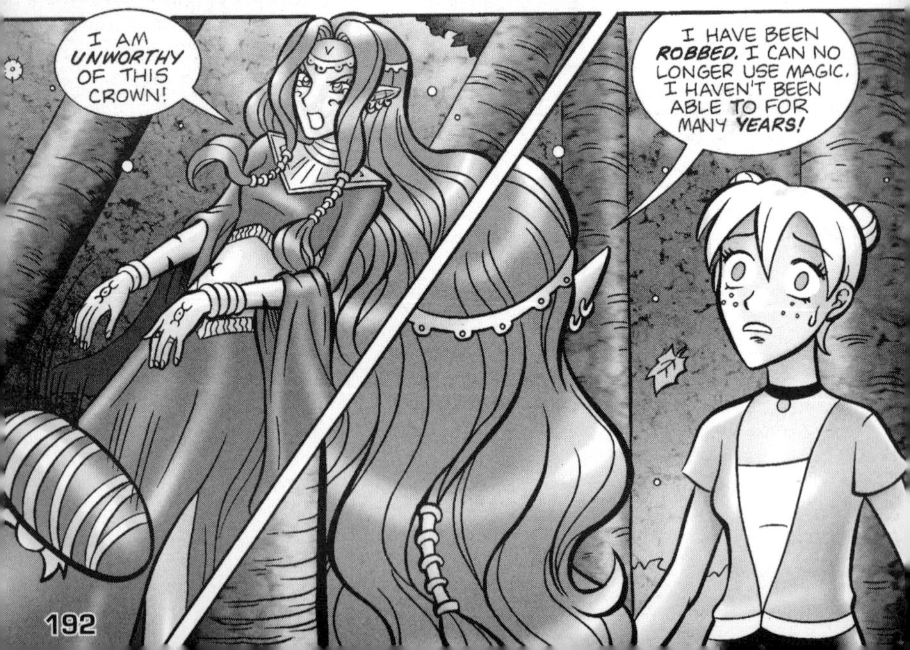
I AM UNWORTHY OF THIS CROWN!
I HAVE BEEN ROBBED. I CAN NO LONGER USE MAGIC. I HAVEN'T BEEN ABLE TO FOR MANY YEARS!

THE **QUEEN** OF THE MAGIC REALM APPEALING TO SABRINA FOR HELP?!

WHAT COULD SHE MEAN BY ALL THIS?

WITH **HEMLOCK** NOW REVEALED AS THE TRAITOR SHE IS, IT'S UP TO **SABRINA**, **SHINJI**, **LLANDRA** AND **NARAYAN** TO UNRAVEL THE MYSTERY IN TIME FOR **FOUR BLADES DAY**!

Chapter 9

The FINAL BATTLE
PART 1
I HAVE BEEN ROBBED. I CAN NO LONGER USE MAGIC. THIS IS WHY YOU--AND THE FOUR BLADES--MUST HELP ME ONCE AGAIN!
WRITER · TANIA DEL RIO
PENCILS · LINDSAY CIBOS
INKS · JIM AMASH
LETTERS · TERESA DAVIDSON
COLORS · JASON JENSEN
EDITOR / MANAGING EDITOR
MIKE PELLERITO
EDITOR-IN-CHIEF
VICTOR GORELICK

I-I DON'T UNDERSTAND! MY BATTY TUTOR TOLD ME THAT THE ORIGINAL FOUR BLADES HAD SWORN TO HELP YOU, BUT IN SCHOOL THEY TEACH US THAT THEY WERE FORMED TO GET RID OF YOU!
I'M SO CONFUSED! THE NEW FOUR BLADES BELIEVE YOU ARE ALLOWING THE REALM TO DIE... HOW CAN WE HELP YOU IF THIS IS TRUE?
I MAY BE ALLOWING THE REALM TO DIE, BUT IT'S NOT BY CHOICE. BELIEVE ME.
LET ME TELL YOU THE TRUE STORY THAT THEY DON'T TEACH YOU IN SCHOOL...
EVEN AS A YOUNG CHILD, I WAS BLESSED WITH MORE MAGICAL SKILL THAN THE AVERAGE WITCH OR WIZARD.
"BUT I WAS AN ORPHAN AND OFTEN FELT VERY ALONE. I DID HAVE MAGICAL FRIENDS SUCH AS THE UNICORNS AND FAERIE FOLK...
"...BUT SOMETIMES I LONGED FOR OTHER CHILDREN TO PLAY WITH.
"THEN ONE DAY I MET A LITTLE BOY WHO DID NOT SEEM TO HAVE A FAMILY EITHER. HE WAS A BIT STRANGE-- HE NEVER TOOK OFF HIS MASK, BUT WE BECAME GOOD FRIENDS."

"EVENTUALLY, I WAS ADOPTED AND GOT TO HAVE MANY ADVENTURES AND SEE MANY EXCITING PLACES. BUT I WAS SAD THAT I HAD TO LEAVE MY FRIEND BEHIND AND OFTEN WONDERED ABOUT HIM.
"HUNDREDS OF YEARS PASSED AND I GAVE UP HOPE OF EVER SEEING MY FRIEND AGAIN. I WAS ELECTED TO THE THRONE HUNDREDS OF YEARS AGO WHILE I WAS STILL VERY YOUNG.
"IT WAS A LOT OF RESPONSIBILITY, BUT THE PEOPLE FELT THAT BECAUSE OF MY MAGICAL SKILLS, AND THE FACT THAT I WAS WELL TRAVELED AND WORLDLY, I WAS THE BEST FIT FOR THE JOB.
"I AM PROUD OF WHAT I HAVE ACHIEVED IN MY TIME. I BROUGHT ABOUT A NEW ERA OF PEACE AND PROSPERITY, AND I, WITH THE HELP OF THE MAGIC COUNCIL, MANAGED TO STOP THE DARK WIZARD, SALEM, FROM TAKING OVER THE REALM MANY YEARS AGO. OUR REALM HAS FLOURISHED SINCE.
"BUT BEING A QUEEN IS LONELY WORK. YOU ARE SURROUNDED BY PEOPLE ALL DAY, BUT FEW SEEM WILLING TO BE A TRUE FRIEND.
"AND THEN, JUST WHEN I NEEDED IT MOST... HE CAME BACK INTO MY LIFE."

"HE TOLD ME HIS NAME WAS ACTUALLY VOSBLANC AND THAT HE REGRETTED HIDING HIS IDENTITY FROM ME WHILE WE WERE CHILDREN.
"HE SAID THAT I WAS HIS ONLY FRIEND IN LIFE AND THAT HE HAD MISSED ME TERRIBLY.
"NEEDLESS TO SAY, I WAS IMMENSELY HAPPY. I FELT LIKE I HAD RE-DISCOVERED THE ONE PERSON, BESIDES MY MOTHER, WHO TREATED ME LIKE A LOVED ONE, AND NOT LIKE A DISTANT QUEEN. I FELT LIKE HE LOVED ME FOR ME. NOT WHO I HAD BECOME...
"I WAS WRONG.
"HE DECEIVED ME.
"HE HAD THE LEGENDARY RARE GEM--THE SOULSTONE--THAT HE HAD ACQUIRED OVER HIS PAST TRAVELS. THE SOULSTONE IS ABLE TO ABSORB MAGIC LIKE A SPONGE AND BESTOW THE PERSON WHO TOUCHES IT WITH SPELLS AND SKILLS OUTSIDE THEIR ABILITIES.
"HE ROBBED ME OF MY POWERS. HE USED THE SOULSTONE TO ABSORB ALL MY SKILLS AND MAGICAL KNOWLEDGE."

SOON THE POWER TO RULE THE MAGIC REALM WILL BE MINE ALONE.
I HAVE THE ROYAL POWER. I AM NOW KING!
I WILL MAKE THEM ACCEPT ME! I WILL RULE THEM BY FORCE!
MAGIC IS ONLY ONE PART OF BEING KING. THE PEOPLE WILL NEVER ACCEPT YOU AS THEIR LEADER! THEY ELECTED ME!
YOU ARE A FOOL IF YOU THINK THAT MY MAGIC ALONE IS ENOUGH TO CONTROL THE ENTIRE REALM. IF ALL THE PEOPLE OF THE REALM BANDED TOGETHER THEY COULD OVERPOWER YOU EASILY. MAGIC IS AN OCEAN AND YOU CAN ONLY CONTROL ONE STREAM!
SILENCE!
BLAST
AAAAGGGH!
BUT SHE IS RIGHT. THE PEOPLE WILL NOT ACCEPT THIS AND CAN FIGHT BACK. I NEED MORE POWER BEFORE I CAN RULE. IF MAGIC IS AN OCEAN, THEN ALL STREAMS FLOW TO ONE PLACE...
THE MANA TREE!

"IN AN EFFORT TO WEAKEN THE MAGIC OF THE PEOPLE AND THE MAGIC OF THE REALM, VOSBLANC BEGAN TO FEED OFF THE MANA TREE ITSELF. SINCE HE HAD MY MAGICAL 'FINGERPRINT' HE WAS ABLE TO ACCESS THE MANA TREE WITHOUT OPPOSITION FROM THE GUARDIANS OF THE FLOATING ISLAND.
ERRGH...
"BUT THE ANCIENT, ETERNAL MANA TREE CONTAINS ALL THE MAGIC OF THE REALM. IT IS FAR TOO MUCH FOR ONE PERSON TO TAKE ALL AT ONCE."
HE BEGAN GOING BACK FREQUENTLY, TAKING ONLY A LITTLE BIT AT A TIME. AT FIRST THERE WAS NO NOTICEABLE IMPACT AND I BEGAN TO FEEL HOPE THAT IT WOULD REMAIN THAT WAY...
"BUT THEN A SINGLE LEAF FELL FROM THE TREE...
"AND I KNEW IT WAS DYING."

IF YOU KNEW THIS WAS GOING ON, WHY DIDN'T YOU TELL ANYONE? HOW COULD YOU LET THE REALM DIE AND KEEP IT A SECRET FROM THE VERY PEOPLE WHO NEED THE MANA TREE TO SURVIVE?
YOU ARE RIGHT, SABRINA. I AM A COWARD.
WITH MY OWN POWERS GONE, I FEEL ASHAMED AND HELPLESS. VOSBLANC IS QUICK TO ANGER, AND I AM AFRAID OF HIM AND WHAT HE IS CAPABLE OF. I HAVE TRIED TO FIGHT HIM ONCE BEFORE, AND FAILED.
HE IS CRUEL. HE HAS THREATENED ME, THAT IF I SHOULD SOUND ANY ALARM, HE WILL ATTACK SCHOOLS AND HOSPITALS WHERE OCCUPANTS ARE NOT STRONG ENOUGH TO FIGHT BACK. AND AS THEIR QUEEN, I WOULD BE POWERLESS TO DEFEND THEM...
PART OF ME FELT THAT AS LONG AS HE WAS QUIETLY OCCUPIED WITH DRINKING FROM THE MANA TREE AND NOT ATTACKING THE REALM DIRECTLY, THERE WAS TIME TO FIGURE OUT A BETTER PLAN. WHICH IS WHERE THE ORIGINAL FOUR BLADES CAME IN.
"I CONFIDED IN TWO OF MY MOST TRUSTED GUARDS, KAJI AND FREYA. I DID NOT TELL THEM THE EXACT NATURE OF MY SITUATION, ONLY THAT VOSBLANC WAS A THREAT WHO NEEDED TO BE DEALT WITH AS DISCREETLY AS POSSIBLE.
"THEY AGREED TO FORM A SECRET, ELITE TEAM TO DEAL WITH VOSBLANC WITHOUT LETTING THE REST OF THE REALM, OR THE MAGIC COUNCIL, KNOW ABOUT IT."

"BUT I UNDERESTIMATED VOSBLANC AND HIS ABILITIES TO TRICK AND DECEIVE.
I MAY BE AN ORDINARY CITIZEN, BUT I HAVE TROUBLING NEWS TO REPORT! THERE IS A SECRET ARMY PREPARING TO OVERTHROW THE QUEEN--AND IT IS SAID THAT SOME OF THE KEY LEADERS ARE MEMBERS OF HER ROYAL GUARD!
DOES THE QUEEN KNOW OF THIS?
PARDON MY THINKING, BUT IT MAY BE BEST THAT SHE IS NOT AWARE--SHE MAY COMPROMISE HER OWN SAFETY. THAT'S WHY I CAME TO YOU, THE CZARINA OF DEFENSE. SURELY YOU, BETTER THAN ANYONE, CAN DEFEND AGAINST THIS THREAT!
"WHILE I WAS FORMING AN ARMY TO FIGHT AGAINST HIM, HE WAS MEETING WITH MEMBERS OF THE COUNCIL TO SPREAD LIES. HE KNEW EXACTLY WHAT TO SAY TO EACH MEMBER TO GET WHAT HE WANTED."
I CAN, AND I WILL! I WILL GET TOGETHER AN ARMY IMMEDIATELY AND STRENGTHEN OUR DEFENSES!
SURELY, BEING THE CZARINA OF DECREE, YOU CAN PREPARE THE PROPER PUNISHMENT FOR THOSE WHO ARE PLOTTING AGAINST THE QUEEN!
HOW DARE THEY! THEY WILL REGRET IT DEARLY! I CAN DO MORE THAN JUST WIPE MEMORIES CLEAN! I WILL BANISH THEM FROM THE REALM! WORSE, EVEN!
AS THE CZARINA OF KNOWLEDGE, IT IS YOUR JOB TO TEACH THE YOUNGSTERS OF THE REALM THE DANGERS OF TREASONOUS THOUGHTS AND ACTS! YOU WILL BE THE VOICE FOR THE NEW GENERATION! WHEN THIS IS DONE, THIS MUST GO IN EVERY TEXTBOOK AND HISTORY CLASS!
YES, YOU CAN TRUST THAT I WILL MAKE IT SO! THANK YOU FOR TELLING ME... WHAT IS YOUR NAME SO THAT WE CAN HONOR YOU IN THE FUTURE TEXTBOOKS?

I NEED NO CREDIT. I DO THIS OUT OF THE GOOD OF MY HEART! FAREWELL, AND GOOD LUCK!
BESIDES, YOU'LL ALL KNOW MY NAME BEFORE TOO LONG. YOU'LL BE WISHING YOU NEVER ASKED!
"MEANWHILE, MY DEAREST GUARD KAJI, THE LEADER OF THE BLADES, LEARNED THE TRUTH BEHIND EVERYTHING... THAT MY MAGICAL POWERS WERE GONE. I DID NOT WANT HIM TO KNOW, BUT HE WAS DRIVEN BY A NEED TO INVESTIGATE, AND HE FOUND OUT."
I KNOW WHAT YOU ARE TRYING TO DO, SELES! AND IT WON'T WORK! YOUR MAGIC BELONGS TO ME NOW! YOU'RE NO BETTER THAN A FILTHY MORTAL! I SHOULD JUST DO AWAY WITH YOU NOW!
"KAJI TRIED TO PUT AN END TO VOSBLANC THEN AND THERE...
BLAST
"...BUT HE WAS NO MATCH AGAINST VOSBLANC'S STRENGTH."

"BUT THIS ONLY CONFIRMED WHAT VOSBLANC HAD WARNED THEM ABOUT... THAT A MEMBER OF THE ROYAL GUARD WAS SAYING TREASONOUS THINGS."
TREASON! HOW DARE YOU SAY SUCH A THING ABOUT OUR QUEEN! YOU ARE THE ONE BEHIND THE ARMY THAT PLANS TO OVERTHROW HER, AREN'T YOU?
"REALIZING HOW DANGEROUS VOSBLANC WAS, KAJI TRIED TO DO WHAT HE THOUGHT WAS RIGHT. HE TOLD THE OTHER COUNCIL MEMBERS MY SECRET... THAT I WAS UNABLE TO USE MAGIC.
N-NO!
GUARDS! SEIZE HIM!
"THIS LED TO THE CHAIN OF EVENTS THAT WOULD EVENTUALLY BE KNOWN AS FOUR BLADES DAY.
"BY THAT TIME, THE MAGIC COUNCIL HAD ALREADY FORMED ITS OWN FORMIDABLE ARMY TO FIGHT BACK, AND THE FOUR BLADES WERE DEFEATED. THROUGH ALL THIS, VOSBLANC WAS NOWHERE TO BE SEEN, BUT HE DIDN'T HAVE TO BE. HE HAD ALREADY PULLED ALL THE STRINGS... ALL HE HAD TO DO WAS SIT BACK AND WATCH THE SHOW."

BY THE END OF THE BATTLE, ALL THE FOUR BLADES HAD EITHER BEEN CAPTURED OR KILLED. KAJI, BEING RECOGNIZED AS THE RINGLEADER, WAS IMPRISONED FOR QUESTIONING.
I KNEW HIS FATE, BUT THERE WAS NOTHING I COULD DO TO HELP HIM. I HAD NO MAGIC TO RELEASE HIS BONDS AND SET HIM FREE.
I AM ASHAMED TO ADMIT THAT AT THE TIME, I WAS ANGRY AT HIM FOR REVEALING MY SECRET, EVEN THOUGH NO ONE BELIEVED HIM.
SOME PART OF ME EVEN BLAMED HIM FOR THE FAILURE OF THE FOUR BLADES. BUT I WAS WRONG. HE RISKED ALL... HE GAVE HIS LIFE FOR ME...
YOU WERE ONE OF MY BEST GUARDS, KAJI, AND I TRUSTED YOU. BUT YOU'RE GOING TO REGRET PRYING. PRAY THAT YOUR CHILDREN DO NOT KNOW THE TRUTH-- FOR THEIR SAKE ALONE. YOU... ARE ALREADY DOOMED.
MY QUEEN, I DID ALL THIS FOR YOU. AND ONE DAY, MY CHILDREN WILL TOO. YOU ARE OUR CHOSEN LEADER AND YOU WILL GET YOUR POWERS BACK. I BELIEVE THAT! THE REALM WILL RETURN TO GREATNESS. WE MAY HAVE LOST THE BATTLE, BUT WE CAN STILL WIN THE WAR.
YOU DID NOT FAIL ME, KAJI. I FAILED YOU.

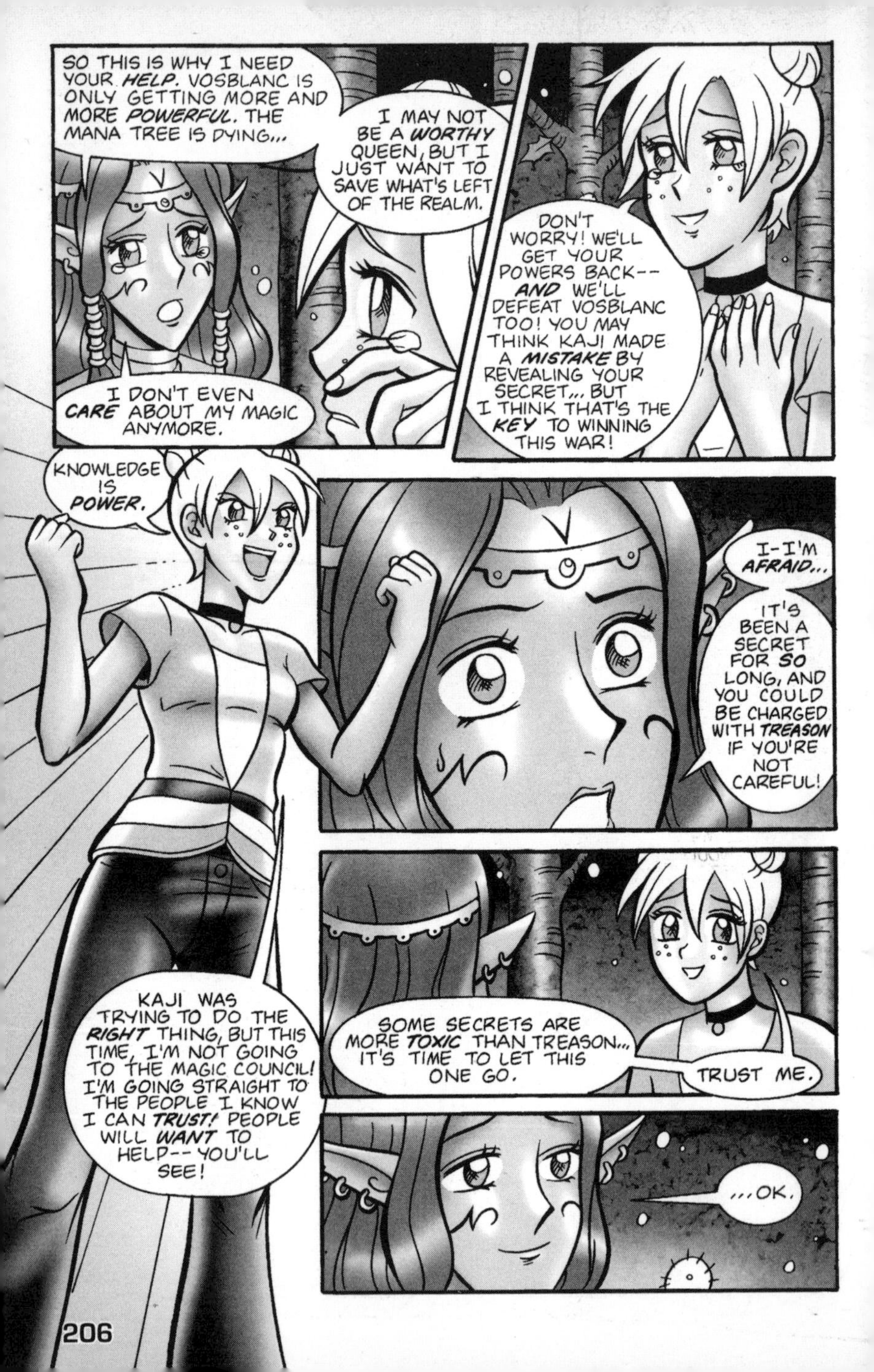

SO THIS IS WHY I NEED YOUR HELP. VOSBLANC IS ONLY GETTING MORE AND MORE POWERFUL. THE MANA TREE IS DYING...
I DON'T EVEN CARE ABOUT MY MAGIC ANYMORE.
I MAY NOT BE A WORTHY QUEEN, BUT I JUST WANT TO SAVE WHAT'S LEFT OF THE REALM.
DON'T WORRY! WE'LL GET YOUR POWERS BACK-- AND WE'LL DEFEAT VOSBLANC TOO! YOU MAY THINK KAJI MADE A MISTAKE BY REVEALING YOUR SECRET... BUT I THINK THAT'S THE KEY TO WINNING THIS WAR!
KNOWLEDGE IS POWER.
I-I'M AFRAID...
IT'S BEEN A SECRET FOR SO LONG, AND YOU COULD BE CHARGED WITH TREASON IF YOU'RE NOT CAREFUL!
KAJI WAS TRYING TO DO THE RIGHT THING, BUT THIS TIME, I'M NOT GOING TO THE MAGIC COUNCIL! I'M GOING STRAIGHT TO THE PEOPLE I KNOW I CAN TRUST! PEOPLE WILL WANT TO HELP-- YOU'LL SEE!
SOME SECRETS ARE MORE TOXIC THAN TREASON... IT'S TIME TO LET THIS ONE GO.
TRUST ME.
...OK.

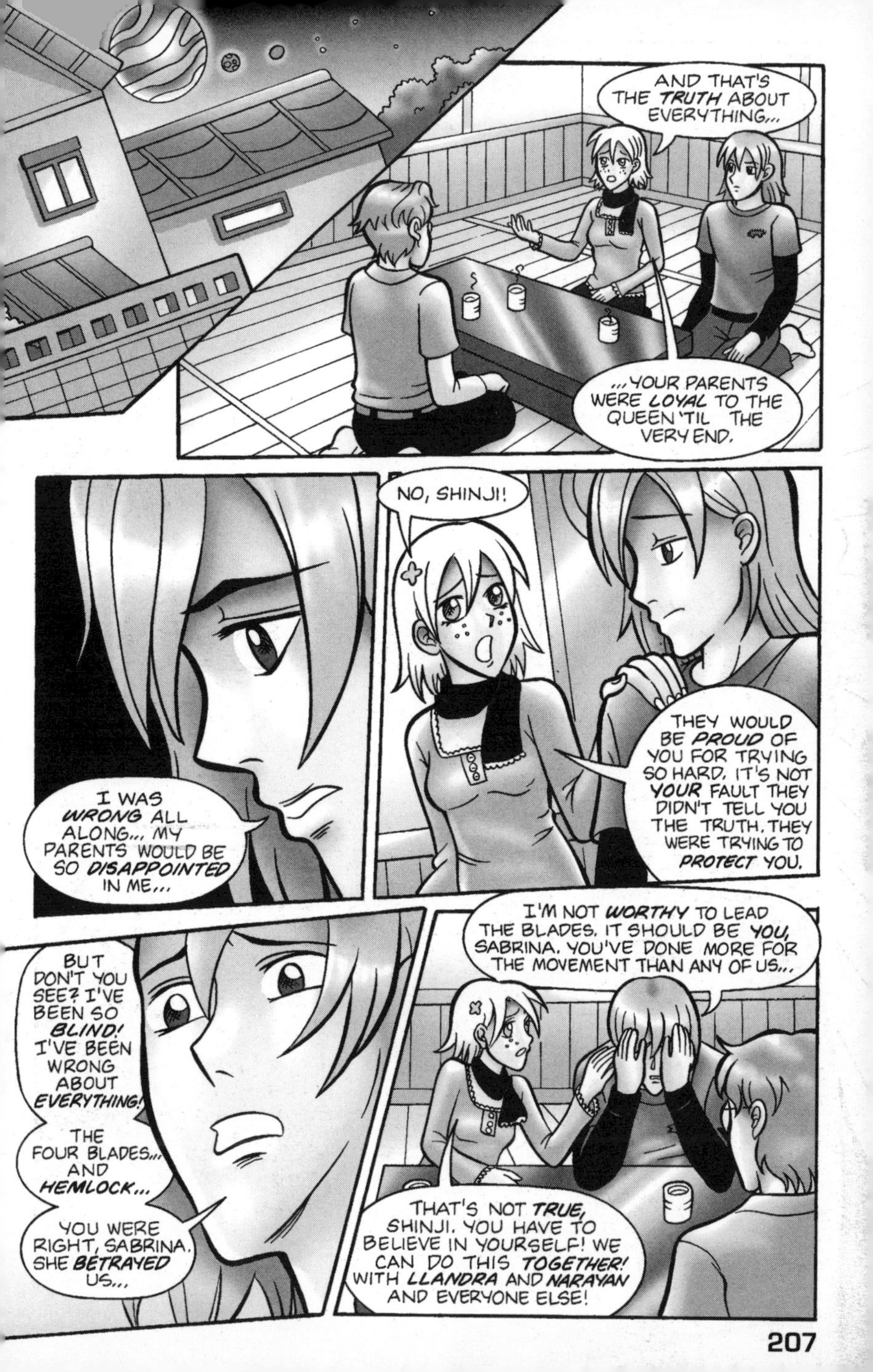
AND THAT'S THE TRUTH ABOUT EVERYTHING...
...YOUR PARENTS WERE LOYAL TO THE QUEEN 'TIL THE VERY END.
I WAS WRONG ALL ALONG... MY PARENTS WOULD BE SO DISAPPOINTED IN ME...
NO, SHINJI!
THEY WOULD BE PROUD OF YOU FOR TRYING SO HARD. IT'S NOT YOUR FAULT THEY DIDN'T TELL YOU THE TRUTH. THEY WERE TRYING TO PROTECT YOU.
BUT DON'T YOU SEE? I'VE BEEN SO BLIND! I'VE BEEN WRONG ABOUT EVERYTHING!
THE FOUR BLADES... AND HEMLOCK...
YOU WERE RIGHT, SABRINA. SHE BETRAYED US...
I'M NOT WORTHY TO LEAD THE BLADES. IT SHOULD BE YOU, SABRINA. YOU'VE DONE MORE FOR THE MOVEMENT THAN ANY OF US...
THAT'S NOT TRUE, SHINJI. YOU HAVE TO BELIEVE IN YOURSELF! WE CAN DO THIS TOGETHER! WITH LLANDRA AND NARAYAN AND EVERYONE ELSE!

WHEN I HEARD WHAT YOU WERE PLOTTING, SHINJI, I WANTED NO PART OF IT, BUT I REALIZE YOUR HEART WAS IN THE RIGHT PLACE. SABRINA IS RIGHT. OUR PARENTS WOULD HAVE WANTED US TO CONTINUE TO GET RID OF VOSBLANC ONCE AND FOR ALL...

KENICHI... DOES THIS MEAN... YOU'RE IN?

ONLY IF YOU'LL CONTINUE TO LEAD THE WAY.

GREAT! NOW, I'D BETTER GET GOING... I STILL HAVE TO TELL EVERYONE ELSE THAT WE KNOW THE TRUTH. STARTING WITH BATTY BARTHOLOMEW AND THE ORIGINAL BLADES!
SABRINA, WAIT.

THANK YOU FOR EVERYTHING.
THAT'S WHAT FRIENDS ARE FOR!
SO, WILL YOU JOIN US NOW? NOW THAT WE KNOW THE TRUTH?
WE THOUGHT YOU'D NEVER ASK!
SO FAR SO GOOD! BUT THERE'S STILL 3 PEOPLE LEFT THAT I NEED TO RECRUIT... AND IT WON'T BE EASY.

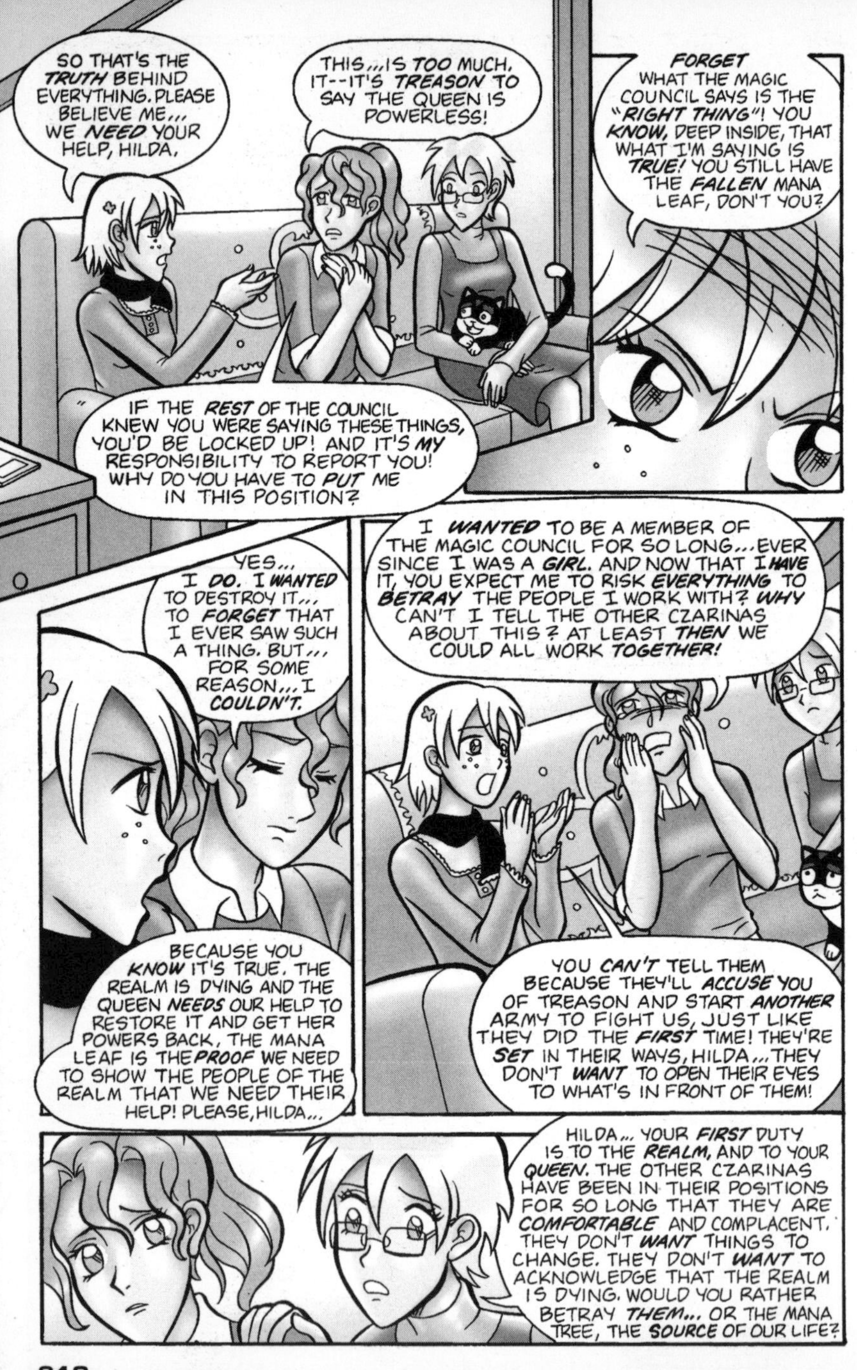
SO THAT'S THE TRUTH BEHIND EVERYTHING. PLEASE BELIEVE ME... WE NEED YOUR HELP, HILDA.
THIS...IS TOO MUCH. IT--IT'S TREASON TO SAY THE QUEEN IS POWERLESS!
IF THE REST OF THE COUNCIL KNEW YOU WERE SAYING THESE THINGS, YOU'D BE LOCKED UP! AND IT'S MY RESPONSIBILITY TO REPORT YOU! WHY DO YOU HAVE TO PUT ME IN THIS POSITION?
FORGET WHAT THE MAGIC COUNCIL SAYS IS THE "RIGHT THING"! YOU KNOW, DEEP INSIDE, THAT WHAT I'M SAYING IS TRUE! YOU STILL HAVE THE FALLEN MANA LEAF, DON'T YOU?
YES... I DO. I WANTED TO DESTROY IT... TO FORGET THAT I EVER SAW SUCH A THING. BUT... FOR SOME REASON... I COULDN'T.
BECAUSE YOU KNOW IT'S TRUE. THE REALM IS DYING AND THE QUEEN NEEDS OUR HELP TO RESTORE IT AND GET HER POWERS BACK. THE MANA LEAF IS THE PROOF WE NEED TO SHOW THE PEOPLE OF THE REALM THAT WE NEED THEIR HELP! PLEASE, HILDA...
I WANTED TO BE A MEMBER OF THE MAGIC COUNCIL FOR SO LONG... EVER SINCE I WAS A GIRL. AND NOW THAT I HAVE IT, YOU EXPECT ME TO RISK EVERYTHING TO BETRAY THE PEOPLE I WORK WITH? WHY CAN'T I TELL THE OTHER CZARINAS ABOUT THIS? AT LEAST THEN WE COULD ALL WORK TOGETHER!
YOU CAN'T TELL THEM BECAUSE THEY'LL ACCUSE YOU OF TREASON AND START ANOTHER ARMY TO FIGHT US, JUST LIKE THEY DID THE FIRST TIME! THEY'RE SET IN THEIR WAYS, HILDA... THEY DON'T WANT TO OPEN THEIR EYES TO WHAT'S IN FRONT OF THEM!
HILDA... YOUR FIRST DUTY IS TO THE REALM, AND TO YOUR QUEEN. THE OTHER CZARINAS HAVE BEEN IN THEIR POSITIONS FOR SO LONG THAT THEY ARE COMFORTABLE AND COMPLACENT. THEY DON'T WANT THINGS TO CHANGE. THEY DON'T WANT TO ACKNOWLEDGE THAT THE REALM IS DYING. WOULD YOU RATHER BETRAY THEM... OR THE MANA TREE, THE SOURCE OF OUR LIFE?

I CAN'T BELIEVE I'M DOING THIS...
LOOK... I MAY NOT BE ABLE TO FIGHT ALONGSIDE YOU, SABRINA... BUT I WILL HELP YOU.
I'LL GIVE YOU ADVICE AND I'LL TRY MY BEST TO KEEP THE OTHER COUNCIL MEMBERS IN THE DARK. TAKE THIS LEAF... AND USE IT. SHOW THE PEOPLE OF THE REALM THE TRUTH.
ALRIGHT, HILDA! WE LOVE YOU!
WOO! THIS IS SO EXCITING AND SCARY!
YEAH! IT'S BEEN SO LONG SINCE WE'VE BEEN IN A GOOD, OLD-FASHIONED, DOWN-HOME MAGICAL BATTLE!
SABRINA, IF WHAT YOU SAY IS TRUE, THIS IS NO TIME FOR CELEBRATION. IF THIS VOSBLANC IS AS STRONG AND AS CUNNING AS YOU'VE MADE HIM OUT TO BE, YOU'RE GOING TO NEED ALL THE HELP YOU CAN GET TO DEFEAT HIM.
OF COURSE... WE'VE GOT ALL THE ORIGINAL MEMBERS OF THE BLADES TO JOIN US... AND WE'LL BE RECRUITING EVEN MORE PEOPLE IN THE DAYS TO COME!
I'M NOT TALKING ABOUT YOUR AVERAGE WITCHES AND WIZARDS. I'M TALKING ABOUT THE ANCIENT POWERS OF THE REALM, THE ELEMENTALS!

"THEY MEET IN THE VALLEY BEYOND THE WIZARDING WASTELANDS... IT WON'T BE EASY. BUT I CAN AT LEAST DRAW THE CURFEW GUARDS AWAY FROM THE AREA FOR SEVERAL DAYS WHILE YOU ENTER. IF THE FOUR OF YOU GO TOGETHER, YOU SHOULD BE ALRIGHT.
"ONCE YOU GET THERE, YOU'LL CALL SYLPH, THE ELEMENTAL OF AIR, DOWN FROM THE FLOATING ISLAND...
"SALAMANDER, THE ELEMENTAL OF FIRE, FROM THE SCORCHED WASTELAND ITSELF...
"UNDINE, THE ELEMENTAL OF WATER, FROM THE OCEAN DEPTHS...
"AND GNOME, THE ELEMENTAL OF EARTH, WHO RESTS IN THE VERDANT VALLEY."

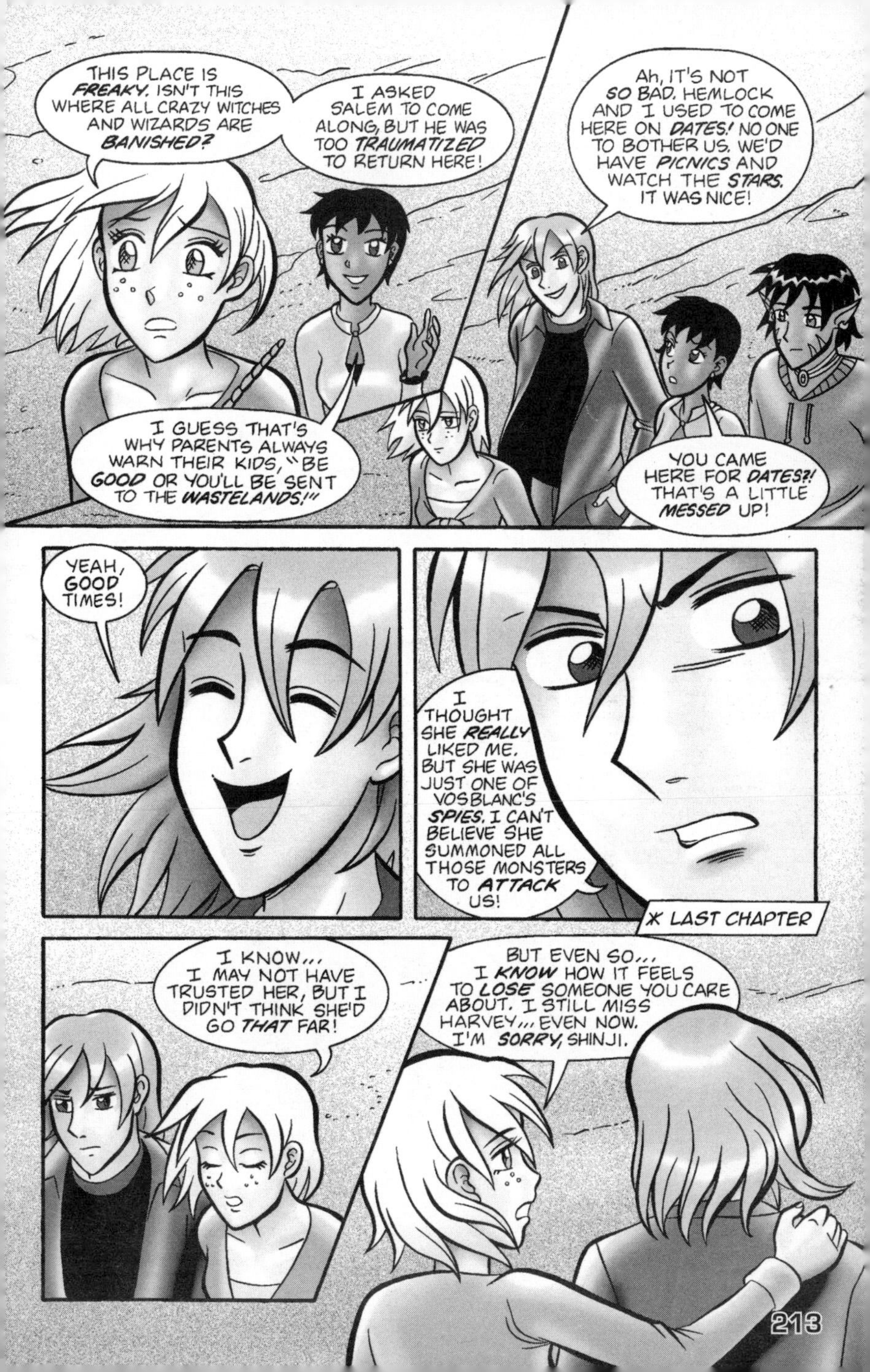
THIS PLACE IS FREAKY. ISN'T THIS WHERE ALL CRAZY WITCHES AND WIZARDS ARE BANISHED?
I ASKED SALEM TO COME ALONG, BUT HE WAS TOO TRAUMATIZED TO RETURN HERE!
I GUESS THAT'S WHY PARENTS ALWAYS WARN THEIR KIDS, "BE GOOD OR YOU'LL BE SENT TO THE WASTELANDS!"
Ah, IT'S NOT SO BAD. HEMLOCK AND I USED TO COME HERE ON DATES! NO ONE TO BOTHER US. WE'D HAVE PICNICS AND WATCH THE STARS. IT WAS NICE!
YOU CAME HERE FOR DATES?! THAT'S A LITTLE MESSED UP!
YEAH, GOOD TIMES!
I THOUGHT SHE REALLY LIKED ME. BUT SHE WAS JUST ONE OF VOSBLANC'S SPIES. I CAN'T BELIEVE SHE SUMMONED ALL THOSE MONSTERS TO ATTACK US!
* LAST CHAPTER
I KNOW... I MAY NOT HAVE TRUSTED HER, BUT I DIDN'T THINK SHE'D GO THAT FAR!
BUT EVEN SO... I KNOW HOW IT FEELS TO LOSE SOMEONE YOU CARE ABOUT. I STILL MISS HARVEY... EVEN NOW. I'M SORRY, SHINJI.

AT LEAST I KNOW WHO MY TRUE FRIENDS ARE...
WHOAA!
BLAST
BLAST
GIT OFFA MY PROPERTY! GO ON, NOW! GIT!
HEY! BACK OFF, WITCH! LET US PASS!
DON'T HURT HER! SHE'S JUST CRAZED AND CONFUSED!
SHE TRIED TO TAKE OUR HEADS OFF!
I MAY NOT HAVE HAD MY LEGS FOR VERY LONG, BUT I THINK I KNOW THE BEST THING TO DO IN A SITUATION LIKE THIS...
RUNNN!!

GASP! I NEED TO LAY OFF THE PIXIE PUFFS!
THERE WERE WAY MORE CRAZY WITCHES AND WIZARDS THAN I EXPECTED.
ALL OF WHOM WERE VERY TERRITORIAL, I MIGHT ADD!
PHEW!
WE MADE IT, GUYS! LOOK!
WOW... I WISH I COULD PAINT THIS. WHO KNEW SUCH A PLACE EXISTED BEYOND THE WASTELANDS?

MEANWHILE...
Y- YOU! THE FUTURE-SEER!
YES. I HAVE RETURNED... AND I FEAR I BEAR THE SAME BAD NEWS AS I DID THE LAST TIME WE MET.
NO DOUBT YOU HAVE HEARD THE RUMORS... THE FOUR BLADES ARE BACK.
AND ONE OF YOUR OWN COUNCILWOMEN IS A MEMBER!
BUT DON'T WORRY... I'M HERE TO HELP. THE FOUR BLADES WILL NEVER GET PAST WHAT I'M PLANNING...

THE BATTLE LINES ARE DRAWN!

WITH THE HELP OF THE ORIGINAL **FOUR BLADES**, HER FAMILY, FRIENDS, AND **THE ELEMENTALS**, CAN SABRINA OVERCOME **VOSBLANC** AND HIS VILLAINOUS ARMY?

Chapter 10

The FINAL BATTLE
PART 2
WRITER/ARTIST • TANIA DEL RIO
INKS • JIM AMASH
LETTERS • TERESA DAVIDSON
COLORS • JASON JENSEN
EDITOR/MANAGING EDITOR • MIKE PELLERITO
EDITOR-IN-CHIEF • VICTOR GORELICK
WE'VE BEEN EXPECTING YOU.
SO YOU KNOW WE'VE COME TO ASK FOR YOUR HELP...

WE ARE THE ELEMENTALS--WE ARE THE COMPLETE EMBODIMENT OF AIR, FIRE, WATER AND EARTH. WE DO NOT LEND OUR AID TO JUST ANYONE.
THEREFORE, YOU WILL EACH HAVE TO EMBARK ON A PERSONAL TEST TO SEE IF YOU CAN MASTER YOUR ELEMENT, AND EACH OF YOU MUST PASS, ON YOUR OWN.
OK, THEN! TELL US WHAT WE HAVE TO DO!

SABRINA, CHILD OF AIR. YOU WILL GO TO THE NORTH AND THERE YOU WILL FIND A TREE. YOU MUST USE THE ELEMENT OF AIR TO BLOW THE FRUIT DOWN FROM THE TREETOP. BRING ME ONE PIECE OF FRUIT FROM ITS BRANCHES.
OK... SOUNDS EASY ENOUGH!
SHINJI, CHILD OF FIRE. TO THE WEST YOU WILL FIND A DEEP CHASM. IN THIS CHASM IS A WOODEN BOX. YOU MUST USE THE ELEMENT OF FIRE TO BURN THE BOX TO REVEAL THE FRUIT WITHIN, BUT TAKE CARE NOT TO SCORCH THE FRUIT ITSELF. THEN BRING IT BACK TO ME.
PIECE OF CAKE!
NARAYAN, CHILD OF WATER. TO THE SOUTH YOU WILL FIND A LAKE. AT THE BOTTOM OF THE LAKE IS A PIECE OF SEA-FRUIT BURIED IN THE MUD. USING THE ELEMENT OF WATER, SWIM AND RETRIEVE THE FRUIT, AND BRING IT BACK TO ME. BUT TAKE CARE, FOR THE SEA-FRUIT MUST REMAIN COVERED IN MUD, FOR IT WILL SHRIVEL IF EXPOSED TO AIR.
I CAN HANDLE IT!

LLANDRA, CHILD OF EARTH. TO THE EAST YOU WILL FIND A PLOT OF LAND AND A BASKET OF SEEDS. YOU MUST PLANT THE SEEDS AND, USING THE ELEMENT OF EARTH, GROW THEM. BRING ME BACK A PIECE OF FRUIT FROM THIS GARDEN.
I CAN DO THAT!
GUYS, THESE CHALLENGES SHOULD BE EASY FOR US.
WE KNOW OUR OWN ELEMENTS LIKE THE BACK OF OUR HANDS! GOOD LUCK!
LET'S DO THIS!

IT'S SOMEWHAT COMFORTING TO SEE THAT EVEN IN THESE DARK TIMES, PEOPLE ARE STILL LOOKING FORWARD TO THE FOUR BLADES HOLIDAY. EVEN WITH THE CURFEW, PEOPLE ARE STILL PLANNING TO PARTY.
FOU
FOUR BLADES DAY PARADE
TOO BAD THEY DON'T REALIZE THAT THERE WON'T BE ANY CAUSE FOR CELEBRATING THIS YEAR.
YEAH... I FEEL BAD. BUT THE TRUTH ABOUT THE QUEEN HAS TO COME OUT.
OOH, OCTOPUS-PIE! CAN WE STOP?
Octo Pie
MAYBE LATER! WE'RE ALREADY RUNNING LATE FOR BATTY BARTHOLOMEW'S MEETING.
Hmmph! YOU CAN'T EXPECT ME TO FIGHT A BATTLE ON AN EMPTY STOMACH! BACK WHEN I WAS TRYING TO TAKE OVER THE WORLD, I ALWAYS MADE SURE I DID SO AFTER A GOOD MEAL!
WE JUST ATE 15 MINUTES AGO! OR HAVE YOU ALREADY FORGOTTEN?! NOW, COME ON!

I'M HOLDING THIS EMERGENCY GATHERING TO DISCUSS SOMETHING OF UTMOST URGENCY.
WAIT, WE CAN'T HOLD A MEETING WITHOUT THE QUEEN PRESENT! AND WHERE IS OUR CZARINA OF CHARITY? WHERE IS BERNADETTE?
THIS IS NOT A FORMAL MEETING. THIS IS SIMPLY AN EMERGENCY GATHERING OF CZARINAS TO DISCUSS SOME TROUBLING DEVELOPMENTS.
VERY WELL, BUT THEN WE SHOULD WAIT FOR BERNADETTE TO ARRIVE.
BERNADETTE WON'T BE COMING. YOU SEE, WE HAVE A TRAITOR IN OUR MIDST, AND ALL SIGNS POINT TO HER.
WHAT?!
BERNIE?
THIS IS MADNESS!
IT IS TRUE. THE FUTURE-SEER HAS VISITED ME ONCE AGAIN. YOU ALL KNOW THAT THE FIRST TIME HE APPEARED HIS WORDS WERE TRUE.
GASP!
THE FUTURE-SEER? WHO IS THAT?
YOU ARE OUR NEWEST COUNCIL MEMBER, SO YOU ARE NOT FAMILIAR WITH HIM. HE HAS NO NAME, BUT HE WARNED US OF THE FIRST FOUR BLADES 12 YEARS AGO. AND HE RECENTLY CAME TO MEET ME AGAIN, BEARING THE SAME WARNING...

THE RUMORS ARE TRUE.
THE FOUR BLADES ARE BACK AND THEY SEEK TO DESTROY THE QUEEN ONCE AND FOR ALL. WORSE, THE FUTURE-SEER TOLD ME THAT ONE OF OUR OWN IS A MEMBER!
HOW DID THEY FIND OUT? I ONLY JUST AGREED LAST NIGHT TO HELP SABRINA AND HER CAUSE. THIS IS ALREADY GETTING WAY OUT OF HAND!*
* LAST CHAPTER
BUT, BERNADETTE? I CAN'T BELIEVE SHE WOULD BETRAY US!
SHE'S BEEN ACTING ODD LATELY. SHE OPPOSED THE CURFEW AND HAS NOT BEEN WILLING TO DISCUSS HOW WE CAN FIGHT BACK AGAINST THE BLADES.
AND I OPPOSED THE CURFEW AS WELL, REMEMBER?
AND I'M CONCERNED AS WELL. IGNACIA, SISTER, WE ALL KNOW BERNIE IS CZARINA OF CHARITY FOR A REASON. SHE HATES WAR AND SUFFERING. SHE WANTS NO PART OF IT! YOU FORGET THAT, BEING THE CZARINA OF DEFENSE!
NOBODY ENJOYS WAR OR SUFFERING, LIBRA! BUT IN TIMES LIKE THESE, YOU ARE EITHER FOR US OR AGAINST US! EVEN THE PACIFISTS!
WHERE IS BERNADETTE NOW? WHY BE SO QUICK TO BLAME HER WHEN ANY ONE OF US HERE COULD BE BLUFFING ABOUT OUR OWN ALLIANCES?
BE VERY CAREFUL HOW YOU APPROACH THIS, HILDA. YOU DIDN'T WANT TO GET TOO INVOLVED, REMEMBER?

BERNIE IS BEING DEALT WITH.
I AM THE OLDEST COUNCIL-MEMBER AND I KNOW EVERYONE HERE CAN BE TRUSTED. EVEN YOU, HILDA. ALTHOUGH YOU HAVEN'T BEEN HERE LONG.
AFTER ALL, YOU ARE IN CHARGE OF ENFORCING THE CURFEW, AND HAVE BEEN DOING A MARVELOUS JOB. IGNACIA HAS BEEN PREPPING OUR DEFENSES, AND SHIMRA HAS BEEN FUNDING THEM. LIBRA HAS ALWAYS BEEN GOOD ABOUT ENSURING THAT THE FOUR BLADES HISTORY IS TAUGHT IN ALL THE MAGIC REALM SCHOOLS, AND SHE WILL CONTINUE TO DO SO ONCE THEY RE-OPEN.
BUT BERNADETTE? WHAT HAS SHE DONE BESIDES OPPOSE OUR EVERY MOVE?
WE CAN'T BE BOGGED DOWN WITH IN-FIGHTING. WE NEED TO FOCUS ON THE TRUE ENEMY! SO WE HAVE TAKEN... PRECAUTIONS TO ENSURE SHE IS REMOVED FROM THE SITUATION UNTIL IT PASSES.
THEY DON'T SUSPECT ME, SO BERNADETTE IS TAKING THE FALL FOR MY OWN ACTIONS. I NEED TO FIND A WAY TO HELP HER OUT OF THIS MESS.
BUT ENOUGH ABOUT THAT.
IF WE ARE GOING TO WIN THIS WAR, WE NEED TO RECRUIT AS MANY WITCHES AND WIZARDS AS WE CAN. AND WHAT BETTER WAY TO DO THAT THAN TO RECRUIT THE CROWDS INVOLVED WITH THE FOUR BLADES FESTIVITIES?
THEY ARE ALREADY LOYAL TO OUR CAUSE, SIMPLY BY THEIR ATTENDANCE!

TOMORROW ARE THE OPENING CEREMONIES. WE WILL BE THERE TO WARN THE CROWD OF THE IMPENDING THREAT AND TO GET THEM INVOLVED!
IF THE FOUR BLADES INTEND TO OVERTHROW THE QUEEN, THEN SHE WILL NEED EXTRA PROTECTION. I WILL VOLUNTEER TO GUARD HER.
EXCELLENT IDEA, HILDA, THE PALACE GUARDS COULD USE SOME ADDITIONAL HELP. I'LL APPOINT SHIMRA AND LIBRA TO ASSIST YOU AS WELL, WHILE IGNACIA AND I DEAL WITH THE CROWDS.
I WAS HOPING TO HAVE THE QUEEN TO MYSELF, BUT PERHAPS THERE WILL BE A WAY TO GET SHIMRA AND LIBRA ON MY SIDE...
MEANWHILE, IN ANOTHER PART OF THE REALM...
FELLOW RENEGADE BLADES! WE HANDED OUT THE GOODIE BAGS! DOES EVERYONE HAVE A FLYING CARPET AND MAGIC MASK? THIS IS GOING TO BE SUCH A FUN COSTUME PARTY!
Um, WHAT BATTY MEANS TO SAY IS THAT WE'LL NEED TO USE THESE TO FIGHT VOSBLANC AND THE MAGIC COUNCIL.

TOMORROW ARE THE OPENING CEREMONIES FOR THE FOUR BLADES FESTIVITIES.
HALF THE MAGIC REALM WILL BE IN ATTENDANCE. THIS WILL BE OUR PERFECT OPPORTUNITY TO SHOW EVERYONE THAT THE REALM IS DYING AND THAT WE NEED THEIR HELP TO RESTORE THE QUEEN'S STOLEN POWERS FROM VOSBLANC!
BUT THINGS COULD GET UGLY! SO BE ON YOUR GUARD AND HAVE THOSE MAGIC MASKS HANDY! ESPECIALLY IF YOU'RE UGLY.
NOW WE WAIT FOR THE FOUR BLADES TO RETURN. HOPEFULLY WITH ELEMENTALS IN TOW...

UGH! I'VE BEEN SEARCHING FOR THIS SO-CALLED TREE FOR AGES, BUT NOTHING IS GROWING HERE IN THE WASTELANDS! ALL I'VE FOUND IS THIS TINY SAPLING, BUT THERE'S NO FRUIT ON IT YET!
IT'S NOT LIKE I CAN JUST SIT HERE AND WAIT FOR IT TO BEAR FRUIT! FOUR BLADES DAY IS TOMORROW!
WHOA.

THIS IS TOO NARROW FOR ME TO CLIMB DOWN.
AND IT LOOKS DEEP TOO!
I CAN'T EVEN SEE THE BOX!
THERE IT IS... BUT HOW AM I SUPPOSED TO GET TO IT?!
THERE'S THE LAKE!
I'LL JUST FIND THE SEA-FRUIT AND BE ON MY WAY!
THAT WAS EASY!

THIS FIELD IS ENORMOUS! AND LOOK AT ALL THESE SEEDS! THIS IS GOING TO TAKE ME FOREVER TO SOW!
UGH!
I WONDER IF I'LL BE THE FIRST ONE BACK? MAYBE THERE'S A SPECIAL PRIZE!
OH, NO! THE MUD IS SLIDING RIGHT OFF THE SEA-FRUIT! IF IT TOUCHES AIR, IT'LL SHRIVEL!
HOW AM I GOING TO GET IT ALL THE WAY BACK TO THE ELEMENTALS WITHOUT THE MUD FALLING OFF?

IF ONLY LLANDRA WAS HERE...
SHE COULD GROW THIS TREE FOR ME IN AN INSTANT, USING HER EARTH-POWERS!
MY FIRE POWERS ARE USELESS IF I CAN'T REACH THE BOX! WHAT AM I SUPPOSED TO DO?

THIS IS RIDICULOUS AND IT'S TAKING FOREVER! IN NATURE, ANIMALS AND WIND HELP SCATTER SEEDS. THIS IS TOO MUCH FOR ONE PERSON ALONE!
WAIT A MINUTE... THAT'S IT!
AND WHAT'S UP WITH THIS "CHASM" ANYWAY? THIS IS A JOKE! THIS ISN'T A CHASM, IT'S A STUPID HOLE IN A GROUND! IT'S A DRIED UP WELL AND MY BOX IS AT THE BOTTOM OF IT!!
A WELL... COULD IT BE?

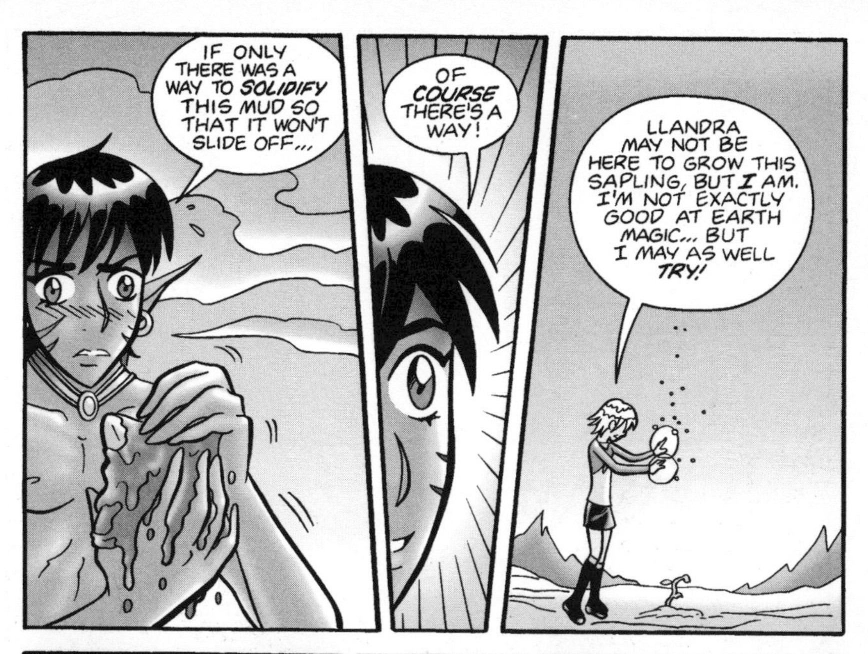
IF ONLY THERE WAS A WAY TO SOLIDIFY THIS MUD SO THAT IT WON'T SLIDE OFF...
OF COURSE THERE'S A WAY!
LLANDRA MAY NOT BE HERE TO GROW THIS SAPLING, BUT I AM. I'M NOT EXACTLY GOOD AT EARTH MAGIC... BUT I MAY AS WELL TRY!

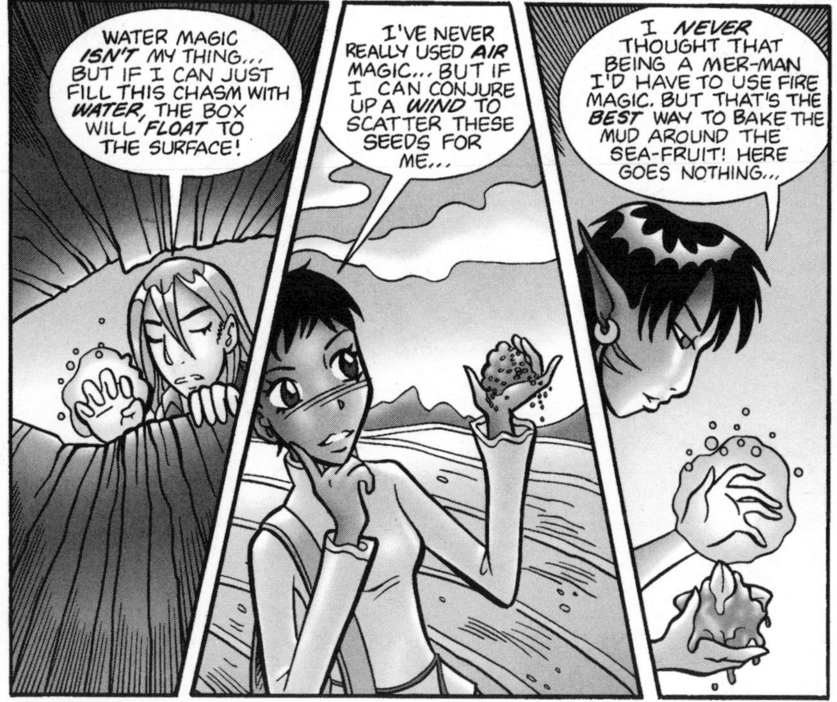
WATER MAGIC ISN'T MY THING... BUT IF I CAN JUST FILL THIS CHASM WITH WATER, THE BOX WILL FLOAT TO THE SURFACE!
I'VE NEVER REALLY USED AIR MAGIC... BUT IF I CAN CONJURE UP A WIND TO SCATTER THESE SEEDS FOR ME...
I NEVER THOUGHT THAT BEING A MER-MAN I'D HAVE TO USE FIRE MAGIC. BUT THAT'S THE BEST WAY TO BAKE THE MUD AROUND THE SEA-FRUIT! HERE GOES NOTHING...

I... CAN'T... DO... THIS!

IT... IT'S WORKING! UNGH!
ERRRGH... ALMOST... THERE!
SO... HOT!
I... CAN... DO... THIS!

AMAZING! YOU HAVE EACH PASSED THE TEST AND HAVE BROUGHT US THE FRUITS OF YOUR LABORS!
AND HOPEFULLY YOU HAVE LEARNED A VALUABLE LESSON IN THE PROCESS.
MASTERING THE ELEMENTS IS MORE THAN JUST MASTERING YOUR OWN ELEMENT.
IT'S ABOUT USING ALL OF THEM TOGETHER-- INCLUDING THE ONES YOU CONSIDER YOUR OPPOSITE!
WE ARE AT YOUR SERVICE. LEAD US TO BATTLE!
FOUR BLADES DAY...
Four Bla

FRIENDS! WE GATHER HERE AS WE DO EACH YEAR TO RECOGNIZE THE HISTORIC EVENT THAT WAS FOUR BLADES DAY...
...WHEN A GROUP OF INDIVIDUALS FOOLISHLY CHALLENGED QUEEN SELES' RIGHT TO THE THRONE! WE DEFEATED THEM THEN... AND WE WILL DEFEAT THEM AGAIN!
AGAIN?
WHAT DOES SHE MEAN?
YOU HAVE NO DOUBT HEARD THE RUMORS. WE ARE HERE TO TELL YOU THAT THEY ARE TRUE! AND THE FOUR BLADES HAVE RETURNED TO FINISH WHAT THEY STARTED!
GASP!
NO!
IS IT TRUE?
WE'LL NEED THE HELP OF EVERY ABLE-BODIED WITCH AND WIZARD TO DEFEAT THIS THREAT ONCE AND FOR ALL! DO NOT BE AFRAID! TOGETHER WE WILL BE VICTORIOUS!
OH, MY GOSH...
HELP US...
WE NEED TO FIGHT!
MMMM
WHAT'S THAT NOISE?
HAS IT ALREADY BEGUN?
!!!

IT'S THEM.
ALREADY?! WE'VE BARELY HAD A CHANCE TO RALLY THE TROOPS!
DO NOT FRET... THIS IS JUST THE FIRST WAVE. MESSENGERS, IF YOU WILL.
WE CAN HOLD THEM OFF FOR NOW.
COWARDS!
DON'T RUN AWAY! FIGHT WITH US!
DON'T CALL OUR CITIZENS COWARDS! THAT'S NO WAY TO GET THEM ON OUR SIDE!
EVERYONE, DON'T BE AFRAID! WE'RE HERE TO HELP YOU, AND WE NEED YOUR HELP IN RETURN!
LOOK AT THIS! IT'S A MANA LEAF! AND IT'S DYING!
IS THAT FOR REAL?
IMPOSSIBLE!
HOW CAN THIS BE?
I'M SCARED!

HEMLOCK!
YOU TOLD ME THAT YOU DESTROYED THE EVIDENCE!
I-I THOUGHT IT WAS TAKEN CARE OF! I WAS CERTAIN THAT SABRINA'S AUNT WOULD DESTROY IT FOR ME!
APPARENTLY, IF YOU WANT SOMETHING DONE, YOU HAVE TO DO IT YOURSELF!
SHOVE
BLAST
SABRINA!
NOOOAAAAGHH!
SHINJI!

ELEMENT OF AIR, CUSHION HIS FALL!
UNNNGHH--
YOU PROMISED ME YOU WOULDN'T HURT SHINJI!
YOU SEEM TO CARE AN AWFUL LOT ABOUT A BOY YOU WERE ONLY PRETENDING TO DATE!
NO, I...I...
OR HAVE YOU FORGOTTEN WHERE YOUR TRUE ALLIANCES LIE?
HE'S DYING! I CAN'T SEEM TO HEAL HIM!
WHAT ABOUT YOUR RESTORATIVE WAND?
YOU CAN DO ANYTHING WITH THAT WAND, SABRINA!
I KNOW! I TRIED! I DON'T KNOW WHY IT WON'T WORK!

BECAUSE, CHILD, YOU DO NOT SEEM TO REALIZE THAT THERE EXIST EVEN GREATER POWERS THAN THOSE WHICH YOU CONTROL. AFTER ALL, ALL YOUR TALENTS ARE JUST A SMALL PORTION OF MY OWN.
WHAT--WHAT IS THAT SUPPOSED TO MEAN?
I AM THE REASON YOUR MAGICAL TALENTS ARE SO STRONG! I GAVE YOU A SLICE OF MY POWER, YOU SEE. AND I, ALONE, CAN HEAL YOUR FRIEND BACK TO HEALTH.
HEAL HIM, THEN! OR ELSE I'LL BLAST YOU!
YOUR WAND WILL HAVE LITTLE EFFECT ON ME, CHILD. DON'T YOU REALIZE HOW POWERFUL I ACTUALLY AM? I DO BELIEVE YOU ARE IN NO POSITION TO BE MAKING THREATS. I, ON THE OTHER HAND, AM WILLING TO OFFER COMPROMISE...
IF YOU HAND OVER THAT MANA LEAF, I WILL CURE THE BOY. A SIMPLE REQUEST, NO?

DON'T... DO... IT, SABRINA. THIS CAUSE IS BIGGER THAN MYSELF. YOU CAN'T... UNGH... GIVE IN!
JUST GIVE HIM THE LEAF, SABRINA! PLEASE! YOU DON'T KNOW WHO YOU'RE DEALING WITH!
WHY SHOULD I LISTEN TO YOU, HEMLOCK? YOU BETRAYED US!
COME, NOW. HAND IT OVER. IS A ROTTING LEAF TRULY WORTH MORE THAN YOUR FRIEND'S LIFE?
SABRINA... PLEASE...
DON'T...
TO BE CONCLUDED!

Chapter 11

The Final Battle
PART 3
COME NOW, SABRINA, HAND OVER THE DYING MANA LEAF AND I WILL HEAL YOUR FRIEND. A FAIR TRADE, DON'T YOU THINK?
D-DON'T DO IT, SABRINA! THAT LEAF... IS THE ONLY PROOF WE HAVE THAT THE MANA TREE IS DYING... THAT THE MAGIC REALM IS DYING! WE NEED IT...
SCRIPT & PENCILS: TANIA DEL RIO
INKS: JIM AMASH
LETTERS: TERESA DAVIDSON
COLORS: JASON JENSEN
EDITOR/MANAGING EDITOR: MIKE PELLERITO
EDITOR-IN-CHIEF: VICTOR GORELICK
I'VE ALREADY LOST HARVEY... I DON'T WANT TO LOSE SHINJI TOO.
THIS IS HIS CAUSE... HE NEEDS TO BE HERE TO SEE IT THROUGH!
I NEED YOU MORE, SHINJI.
FINE. TAKE IT. NOW HEAL SHINJI!

HEAL HIM?
DID I SAY "HEAL HIM"? I MEANT TO SAY...
FSSSSSSS
...PUT HIM OUT OF HIS MISERY!
ELEMENTAL OF AIR! SHIELD US!
I... CAN'T... HOLD IT... FOR LONG!
VOSBLANC!! STOP IT!

HOW DARE YOU? WHOSE SIDE ARE YOU ON, HEMLOCK?!
I WANT TO BE YOUR QUEEN, BUT YOU PROMISED NOT TO HURT SHINJI!
THIS IS WAR! AND PEOPLE WILL DIE WHETHER YOU LIKE IT OR NOT!
WHAT IS ALL THIS "QUEEN" TALK? QUEEN SELES IS SAFELY HIDDEN AWAY, AND WE'RE HERE TO PROTECT HER FROM THE FOUR BLADES, REMEMBER? YOU SAID YOU WOULD HELP US DEFEAT THEM!
WHAT ARE WE WAITING FOR? OUR PEOPLE ARE READY TO FIGHT!
GALIENA, MY DEAR, WE'RE JUST GETTING WARMED UP.
YOU'RE TOO WEAK TO BE MY QUEEN.
AND YOU'RE TOO FOOLISH TO REALIZE I NEVER INTENDED TO MAKE YOU ONE, ANYWAY!
GET HIM AND HEMLOCK SOMEWHERE SAFE, NARAYAN, AND CALL THE REST OF THE RENEGADE BLADES! THE REAL BATTLE IS ABOUT TO BEGIN!

ENOUGH OF THIS NONSENSE! I WANT TO BE OUTSIDE! I WANT TO KNOW WHAT'S HAPPENING!
QUEEN SELES, FORGIVE US, BUT WE'VE BEEN ORDERED TO PROTECT YOU!
ORDERED BY WHOM? I AM THE QUEEN!
YOUR HIGHNESS, THE FOUR BLADES HAVE RETURNED AND THEY ARE TRYING TO OVERTHROW YOU ONCE AGAIN.
OUR ARMIES ARE ALL OUTSIDE READY TO DESTROY THEM--IT'S BEST THAT WE WAIT HERE!
I DON'T WANT THE FOUR BLADES TO BE DESTROYED, AND NEITHER DOES HILDA. ISN'T THAT RIGHT, CZARINA?
IT'S TRUE... MY NIECE, SABRINA, IS ONE OF THE FOUR BLADES. AND I'M VERY CONCERNED ABOUT HER...

YOU! YOU ARE THE TRAITOR AMONG US, NOT BERNADETTE!
YOU KNEW ABOUT SABRINA'S INVOLVEMENT AND DIDN'T SAY ANYTHING!
BECAUSE HER CAUSE IS JUST!
GALIENA HAS MISLED YOU! THE FOUR BLADES AREN'T TRYING TO HURT THE QUEEN-- THEY'RE TRYING TO HELP HER!
PLEASE STOP THIS! WHAT HILDA SAYS IS TRUE! I ASKED THE FOUR BLADES TO HELP ME RESTORE THE POWERS THAT WERE STOLEN FROM ME! THEY'RE ON MY SIDE!
I CAN'T MAKE SENSE OF THIS! WHO ARE WE TO BELIEVE?!
BELIEVE ME. PLEASE. WE NEED TO HELP THE FOUR BLADES BEFORE MY ARMIES CAN DESTROY THEM!
LOOK, I'LL EXPLAIN ON THE WAY. BUT FIRST WE NEED TO FREE BERNADETTE. SHE'S BEEN HELD SOMEWHERE IN THE BUILDING EVER SINCE SHE WAS ACCUSED OF BEING A TRAITOR.
I KNOW WHERE SHE IS. LET'S GO!

CITIZENS! DON'T RUN AWAY! HELP US FIGHT AND MAKE HISTORY ONCE AGAIN! FIGHT TO SAVE YOUR QUEEN!
DON'T LISTEN TO HER LIES! WE'RE ON THE QUEEN'S SIDE! THE MANA TREE IS DYING AND VOSBLANC IS RESPONSIBLE!
HAHAHAHAHA! PROVE IT!

HE'S RIGHT! NOW THAT THE LEAF IS DESTROYED WE HAVE NO WAY TO SHOW THE PEOPLE THAT WHAT WE SAY IS TRUE! WE DID MANAGE TO SWAY A FEW, BUT WE'RE STILL OUTNUMBERED!
DODGE
CURSE THOSE FLYING CARPETS! IT'S TOO HARD TO HIT A MOVING TARGET! WE NEED TO GET THEM ONTO THE GROUND!
VERY WELL... RELEASE THE HOUNDS!
GRRRR

USE YOUR MASKS!
OOH, A MASQUERADE! MY FAVORITE PART OF ANY BALL!

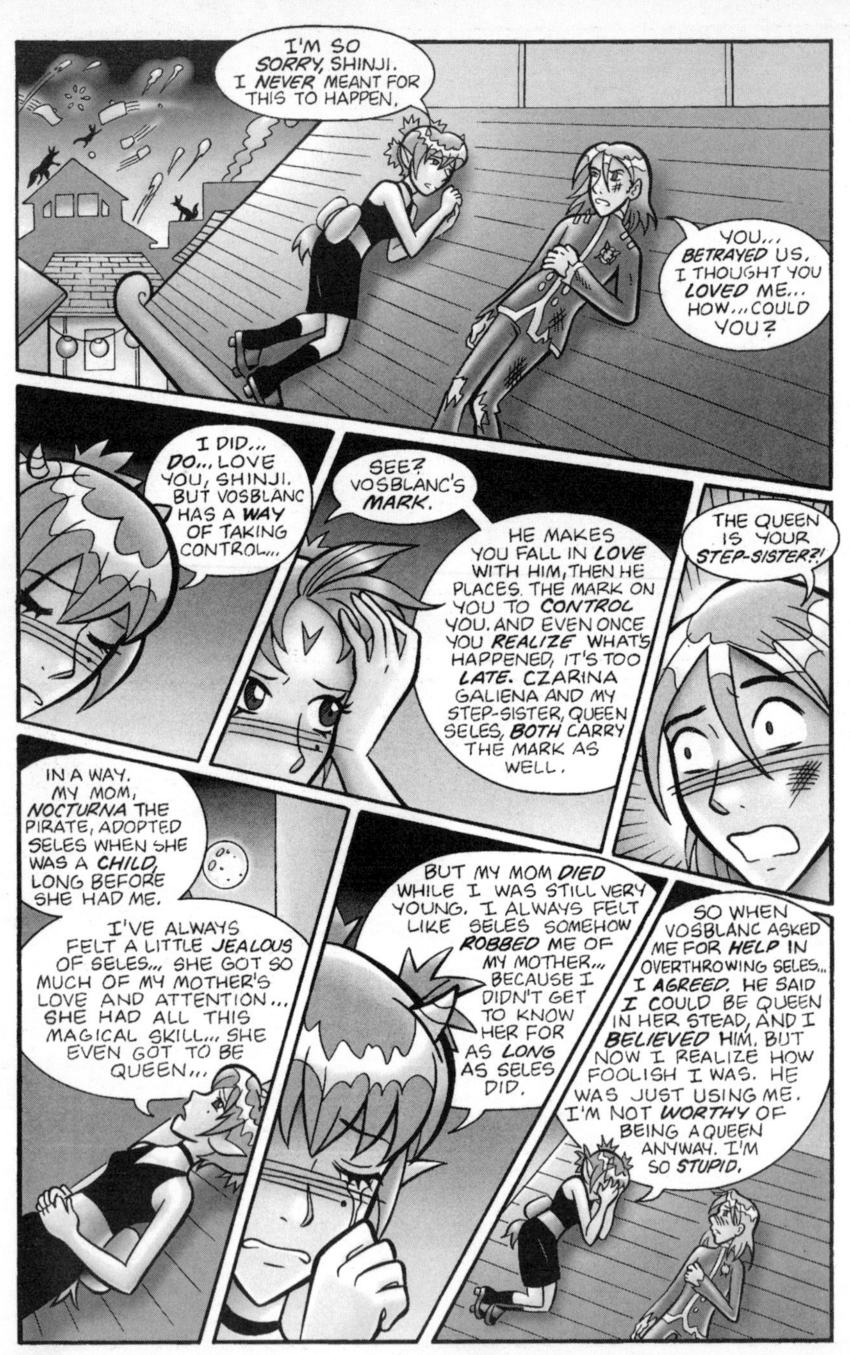
I'M SO SORRY, SHINJI. I NEVER MEANT FOR THIS TO HAPPEN.
YOU... BETRAYED US. I THOUGHT YOU LOVED ME... HOW... COULD YOU?
I DID... DO... LOVE YOU, SHINJI. BUT VOSBLANC HAS A WAY OF TAKING CONTROL...
SEE? VOSBLANC'S MARK.
HE MAKES YOU FALL IN LOVE WITH HIM, THEN HE PLACES. THE MARK ON YOU TO CONTROL YOU. AND EVEN ONCE YOU REALIZE WHAT'S HAPPENED, IT'S TOO LATE. CZARINA GALIENA AND MY STEP-SISTER, QUEEN SELES, BOTH CARRY THE MARK AS WELL.
THE QUEEN IS YOUR STEP-SISTER?!
IN A WAY. MY MOM, NOCTURNA THE PIRATE, ADOPTED SELES WHEN SHE WAS A CHILD, LONG BEFORE SHE HAD ME.
I'VE ALWAYS FELT A LITTLE JEALOUS OF SELES... SHE GOT SO MUCH OF MY MOTHER'S LOVE AND ATTENTION... SHE HAD ALL THIS MAGICAL SKILL... SHE EVEN GOT TO BE QUEEN...
BUT MY MOM DIED WHILE I WAS STILL VERY YOUNG. I ALWAYS FELT LIKE SELES SOMEHOW ROBBED ME OF MY MOTHER... BECAUSE I DIDN'T GET TO KNOW HER FOR AS LONG AS SELES DID.
SO WHEN VOSBLANC ASKED ME FOR HELP IN OVERTHROWING SELES... I AGREED. HE SAID I COULD BE QUEEN IN HER STEAD, AND I BELIEVED HIM. BUT NOW I REALIZE HOW FOOLISH I WAS. HE WAS JUST USING ME. I'M NOT WORTHY OF BEING A QUEEN ANYWAY. I'M SO STUPID.

YOU'RE NOT STUPID... WE ALL MAKE MISTAKES. ESPECIALLY WHEN IT COMES TO LOVE. I GUESS YOU COULD SAY I BETRAYED YOU AS WELL.
WHAT DO YOU MEAN?

EVEN WHILE WE WERE TOGETHER... I KNEW MY HEART WASN'T IN IT. I'VE ALWAYS LOVED SABRINA... I'M SORRY, HEMLOCK.

I FIGURED AS MUCH.

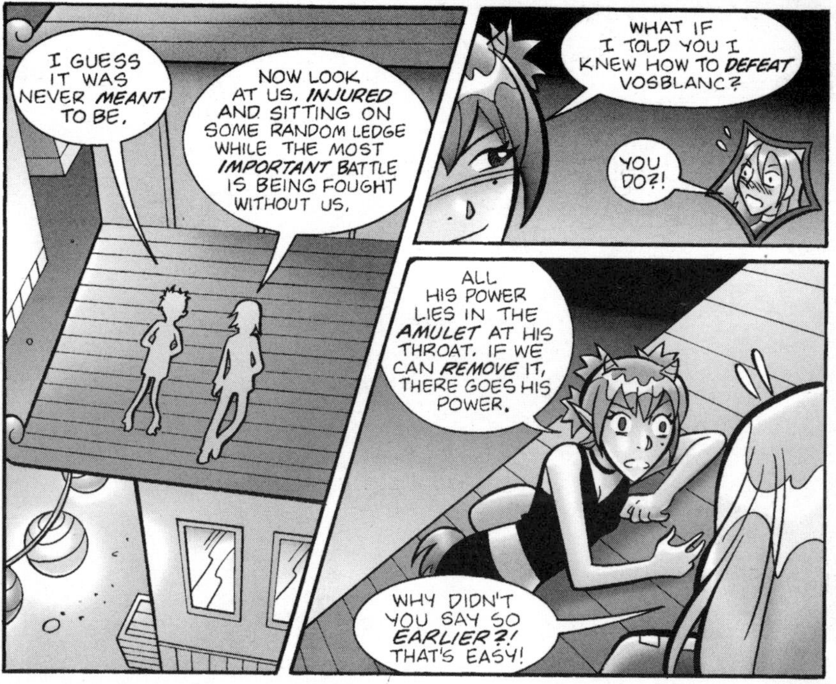
I GUESS IT WAS NEVER MEANT TO BE.
NOW LOOK AT US. INJURED AND SITTING ON SOME RANDOM LEDGE WHILE THE MOST IMPORTANT BATTLE IS BEING FOUGHT WITHOUT US.
WHAT IF I TOLD YOU I KNEW HOW TO DEFEAT VOSBLANC?
YOU DO?!
ALL HIS POWER LIES IN THE AMULET AT HIS THROAT. IF WE CAN REMOVE IT, THERE GOES HIS POWER.
WHY DIDN'T YOU SAY SO EARLIER?! THAT'S EASY!

NOT QUITE.
THE AMULET HAS A STRONG BOND WITH VOSBLANC. WHOEVER BREAKS IT WOULD BE CAUGHT DIRECTLY IN THE MAGICAL FISSURE. IT WOULD... KILL THEM.
LOOK AT ME, HEMLOCK. I'M ALREADY DYING. IF THIS IS THE LAST THING I CAN DO, THEN IT WILL ALL BE WORTH IT. WILL YOU HELP ME?
AS LONG AS I HAVE THIS MARK, FIGHTING AGAINST VOSBLANC WILL BE REALLY DIFFICULT. EVEN SHOVING HIM EARLIER TOOK ALL MY WILLPOWER.
BUT I PROMISE TO DO WHATEVER I CAN, SHINJI.
HE HAS TO BE STOPPED!
HANSEL, PLEASE!
I DON'T WANT TO HURT YOU!
I DON'T WANT TO HURT YOU EITHER! BUT I CAN'T LET YOU OVERTHROW THE QUEEN!
WELL, SO AM I!
BLAST
I'M NOT TRYING TO OVERTHROW THE QUEEN! I'M TRYING TO HELP HER!

ENOUGH OF THIS FIGHTING AND DESTRUCTION! DON'T YOU SEE?
WE'RE ALL ON THE SAME SIDE! WE ALL WANT THE QUEEN AND THE REALM TO SURVIVE! THE MANA TREE IS DYING AS WE SPEAK, AND WE'RE DOWN HERE FIGHTING! FOR WHAT?!
BLASPHEMY! THE MANA TREE CAN'T DIE! IT'S IMMORTAL!
BLASPHEMY, INDEED! THIS IS THE KIND OF TALK WE CANNOT ALLOW IN OUR REALM! TO SAY THE MANA TREE IS DYING IS TO SAY THE QUEEN IS A FARCE!
I AM A FARCE! SABRINA SPEAKS TRUE--
--THE TREE IS DYING, AND SO IS THE REALM. MY MAGIC HAS BEEN ROBBED--AND SO HAS YOURS!
S-SELES? WHAT IS THE MEANING OF THIS? HAVE YOU BETRAYED US?
NO! HE HAS! HE KILLED TREE!
YOU CAN SAY WHATEVER YOU LIKE ABOUT THE MANA TREE! YOU HAVE NO PROOF!
IT'S A THOUSAND MILES ABOVE US, ON A FLOATING ISLAND, PROTECTED BY THE ELEMENTAL SYLPHANARI.

YEAH? WELL, SYLPHANARI AND I ARE LIKE THIS.
YOU WANT PROOF? WE'LL BRING IT TO YOU!
WHAT? IMPOSSIBLE!
SYLPHANARI, ELEMENTAL OF AIR! AID ME!
AS ABOVE, SO BELOW!
GASP!
SABRINA! OH MY GOSH...
LOOK!

THE MANA TREE!
SLAM
IT'S WITHERED!
SHE WAS TELLING THE TRUTH!
HOW COULD SHE--!!

VERY IMPRESSIVE, SABRINA. YOU'VE PROVED YOUR POINT! BUT SO WHAT? THE TREE IS ALL BUT DEAD! AND SOON ALL THIS REALM'S MAGIC WILL DRY OUT COMPLETELY!
AND WHAT OF YOU? WHAT GOOD WILL IT DO YOU TO RULE OVER A DEAD REALM? WHAT'S THE POINT?
YOU THINK I WANT TO RULE THE MAGIC REALM? HA! MY AMBITIONS ARE MUCH BIGGER THAN THAT. NO, I SIMPLY WANTED TO ABSORB ALL THE MAGIC IN THE REALM SO THAT I CAN BE POWERFUL ENOUGH...
...TO TAKE OVER THE MORTAL WORLD!
NO! THE MORTALS WOULD BE POWERLESS AGAINST HIS MAGIC!
IN FACT, I DO BELIEVE I'VE OVERSTAYED MY WELCOME HERE! I THINK I HAVE MORE THAN ENOUGH POWER TO BEGIN WORK ON THE MORTAL REALM!
SHOOM
BUT FIRST-- A PARTING GIFT!
BLAST
NOOOOO!!
SOB!
HOW COULD YOU?!
SOB!
SOB!

HE'S ABOUT TO ESCAPE! WE CAN'T LET THAT HAPPEN!
HURRY! HELP ME GET CLOSER AND I'LL GRAB HIS AMULET!
ARE YOU SURE ABOUT THIS, SHINJI?
YES. JUST...
...TELL SABRINA THAT I LOVE HER... WILL YOU?
NO.
--NO?
THAT SORT OF THING... YOU SHOULD TELL HER YOURSELF.
HEMLOCK! NOoo! YOUR MARK! IT WON'T LET YOU!

NO STUPID MARK IS GOING TO TELL ME HOW TO LIVE! MY LIFE IS IN MY OWN HANDS!
TMP!
KRAK
MY AMULET!! MY POWERS!
I DON'T THINK SO.
SLIDE

KIT!?
JUST FIGURED IT OUT, huh?
WELL, IT TOOK ME A WHILE TO PIECE IT TOGETHER AS WELL.
WE MET IN THE MAGICAL FOREST MANY MONTHS AGO AND YOU HELPED ME RETRIEVE MY LOST AMULET.
LITTLE DID I KNOW THAT BY TOUCHING IT, SOME OF ITS POWER WOULD TRANSFER TO YOU.
YOU THOUGHT ALL YOUR MARVELOUS POWERS WERE BECAUSE YOU WERE SPECIAL, huh?
YOUR INVENTING NEW SPELLS, GIVING MERMEN LEGS, RETRIEVING MEMORIES. IT WAS JUST YOU ABUSING THE POWER THAT I STOLE FROM THE MANA TREE!
HAVEN'T YOU DONE ENOUGH DAMAGE ALREADY?
LOCK HIM UP!
I DON'T THINK SO! I MAY NOT HAVE MY POWERS, BUT I STILL HAVE MY WITS!
JUMP
HE GOT AWAY!
BUT HE'S POWERLESS. HE WON'T BE ABLE TO HIDE FOR LONG.
SHOOP

I MISJUDGED HEMLOCK. I'M SO SORRY, SHINJI. I KNOW HOW MUCH YOU CARED ABOUT HER. SHE SAVED US.
I DID CARE ABOUT HER... BUT SHE GAVE HER LIFE SO I COULD TELL YOU SOMETHING...
I LOVE YOU, SABRINA, AND WE COULDN'T HAVE DEFEATED VOSBLANC WITHOUT YOUR HELP, AND YOUR AMAZING MAGIC.
MY STOLEN MAGIC. OH, WHAT'S THE POINT, SHINJI? THE MANA TREE IS DEAD, THE REALM IS DESTROYED...
OH, LITTLE SISTER. THIS IS ALL MY FAULT. I SHOULD HAVE ASKED FOR HELP SOONER.
I SHOULD HAVE TOLD MY CITIZENS THE TRUTH... THAT MY MAGIC WAS ROBBED OF ME. I WAS TOO PROUD. AND NOW THE REALM... AND YOU... ARE DEAD BECAUSE OF IT.

HERE, SELES. YOUR POWERS, RETURNED.
NO. I'M NOT WORTHY OF THIS MAGIC. YOU, SABRINA, SHOULD TAKE IT AND BECOME OUR NEXT QUEEN.

M-ME? THE QUEEN?
YOU DESERVE IT, SABRINA. YOU CAN HELP US HEAL THE REALM.
SHE'S RIGHT, SABRINA!
WAIT... DOES THIS MEAN SHE WON'T CLEAN MY HOUSE ANYMORE?
NO. THIS MAGIC DOESN'T BELONG TO ME. IT BELONGS TO EVERYONE HERE. IT BELONGS TO THE REALM.

BURY
SHINJI? LLANDRA? NARAYAN? I NEED YOUR HELP.
TODAY BEGINS AN ERA OF CHANGE. WE ARE NO LONGER THE FOUR BLADES-- BLADES BEING WEAPONS OF DESTRUCTION.
WE'RE NOW THE FOUR BLADES OF GRASS--BLADES OF GROWTH AND RENEWAL.
A NEW MANA TREE WILL GROW RIGHT HERE, IN THE PLAZA, WHERE EVERYONE CAN ENJOY IT AND NURTURE IT--NOT ON SOME FLOATING ISLAND FAR AWAY.
WE'LL ALL REBUILD THE REALM! IT WILL TAKE TIME, BUT WE CAN DO IT! TOGETHER!

Thanks to all my readers + fans for following Sabrina's manga adventures! I hope you enjoyed it! I'd like to thank Jim, Teresa + Jason for making the book look amazing. I also want to thank all the awesome people at Archie - especially Mike Pellerito + Victor Gorelick!!

Love,
Tania del Rio
1/9/09

FIRST SABRINA
INITIAL MANGA
CHARACTER DESIGN
BY TANIA DEL RIO
Bonus Page

ANOTHER EARLY SABRINA PENCIL DRAWING BY TANIA
Bonus Page

POSTCARD PROMO SKETCH
What's a witch to do?
who says magic can solve problems?
The Council
The Crushes
The Cat
what's a witch to do when just spells aren't enough?
what's a witch to do when magic won't do the trick?
Bonus Page

UNUSED ROUGH COVER SKETCH
#71
1 of 3
SABRINA
snow!
Strawberry lip gloss
Strawberry Lip Gloss
Bonus Page

UNUSED ROUGH COVER SKETCH
SABRINA
THE TEENAGE WITCH
サブリナ
Bonus Page

UNUSED ROUGH COVER SKETCH
SABRINA
サブリナ
Bonus Page

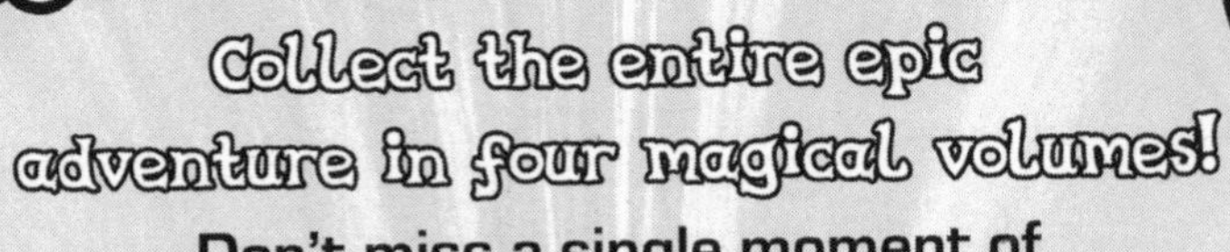

Don't miss a single moment of
Sabrina the Teenage Witch: The Magic Within
from Archie COMICS!

Sabrina:
The Magic Within 1

January 2013

ISBN:
978-1-936975-39-6

Sabrina:
The Magic Within 2

June 2013

ISBN:
978-1-936975-54-9

Sabrina:
The Magic Within 3

September 2013

ISBN:
978-1-936975-60-0

Sabrina:
The Magic Within 4

December 2013

ISBN:
978-1-936975-76-1

FIND THESE AND MORE GREAT ARCHIE BOOKS AT COMIC SHOPS, BOOKSTORES, AND ARCHIECOMICS.COM!